A Gift of Three

A Shade of Vampire, Book 42

Bella Forrest

ALSO BY BELLA FORREST:

THE SECRET OF SPELLSHADOW MANOR

The Secret of Spellshadow
Manor (Book 1)
The Breaker (Book 2)

THE GENDER GAME

The Gender Game (Book 1)
The Gender Secret (Book 2)
The Gender Lie (Book 3)
The Gender War (Book 4)
The Gender Fall (Book 5)

A SHADE OF VAMPIRE SERIES:

Series 1:
Derek & Sofia's story:

A Shade of Vampire (Book 1)
A Shade of Blood (Book 2)
A Castle of Sand (Book 3)
A Shadow of Light (Book 4)
A Blaze of Sun (Book 5)
A Gate of Night (Book 6)
A Break of Day (Book 7)

Series 2:
Rose & Caleb's story:

A Shade of Novak (Book 8)
A Bond of Blood (Book 9)
A Spell of Time (Book 10)
A Chase of Prey (Book 11)
A Shade of Doubt (Book 12)
A Turn of Tides (Book 13)
A Dawn of Strength (Book 14)
A Fall of Secrets (Book 15)
An End of Night (Book 16)

Series 3: The Shade continues with a new hero...

A Wind of Change (Book 17)
A Trail of Echoes (Book 18)
A Soldier of Shadows (Book 19)
A Hero of Realms (Book 20)
A Vial of Life (Book 21)
A Fork Of Paths (Book 22)
A Flight of Souls (Book 23)
A Bridge of Stars (Book 24)

Series 4:
A Clan of Novaks

A Clan of Novaks (Book 25)
A World of New (Book 26)
A Web of Lies (Book 27)
A Touch of Truth (Book 28)

An Hour of Need (Book 29)
A Game of Risk (Book 30)
A Twist of Fates (Book 31)
A Day of Glory (Book 32)

Series 5:
A Dawn of Guardians

A Dawn of Guardians (Book 33)
A Sword of Chance (Book 34)
A Race of Trials (Book 35)
A King of Shadow (Book 36)
An Empire of Stones (Book 37)
A Power of Old (Book 38)
A Rip of Realms (Book 39)
A Throne of Fire (Book 40)
A Tide of War (Book 41)

A SHADE OF DRAGON TRILOGY :

A Shade of Dragon 1
A Shade of Dragon 2
A Shade of Dragon 3

A SHADE OF KIEV TRILOGY:

A Shade of Kiev 1
A Shade of Kiev 2
A Shade of Kiev 3

DETECTIVE ERIN BOND
(Adult mystery/thriller)

Lights, Camera, Gone
Write, Edit, Kill

BEAUTIFUL MONSTER DUOLOGY:

Beautiful Monster 1
Beautiful Monster 2

For an updated list of Bella's books, please visit her website:
www.bellaforrest.net

Join Bella's VIP email list and she'll personally send you an email
reminder as soon as her next book is out! Visit here to sign up:
www.forrestbooks.com

Contents

HAZEL

I leaned back against my husband's chest, sighing with contentment as I surveyed the waves gently lapping against the shoreline. Moonbeams danced across the black waters, their rays like shimmering spotlights over The Shade.

It was almost eight months since we'd returned from Nevertide, and already a lot had changed. I drew my hand across my stomach, my fingertips idly flitting over the bump—it was something I did often, preoccupied with the strange sensation of having my body changed so much by the child growing inside me. Our child.

It was still early in the pregnancy, but sometimes the

baby would give me a small kick, making me aware of its presence, making me feel like a *mom*, which was mind-blowingly surreal and wonderful all at once. Apparently, supernatural babies showed more early activity than human ones.

"Are you cold?" Tejus asked me, wrapping his arms around my frame without waiting for a reply. As always, his embrace made me feel secure—like our little family unit, just me, Tejus and the bump, was indestructible.

"I'm not cold at all." I smiled. "But this is good."

"How's the bump?"

I chuckled. "Active today… quite a few little kicks."

I didn't need to turn around to know that my husband was grinning from ear to ear. He was just as excited about the birth as I was, already planning on how to turn a room in our treehouse into a nursery, and studying birthing books like he was preparing for an exam. I'd told him that Corrine would be on hand throughout the delivery and afterwards, along with my mother and my grandmother—there would be plenty of experts—but he wouldn't listen. The astute, strategic mindset he had once used to organize armies in Nevertide, and lately GASP missions, he now focused on the birth of our child, studying everything in painstaking detail.

"It's around week sixteen, that sounds about right," the 'expert' replied.

I laughed, taking Tejus's hands in mine. I placed them on my stomach and he rubbed my skin gently over my t-shirt. We stayed like that, in silence, for a while—just listening to the waves, and the crackle of the fire that Tejus had built next to us.

I started to daydream, picturing what life would be like with our child, what our 'bump' might grow to be like, to look like—dark hair was a given, and so was pale skin. Sentry skills were to be expected; this had been confirmed by Corrine. It made me smile. Our half-ghoul child…it was such a weird concept.

"How was training, by the way?" I asked eventually, coming back to the present.

Tejus, Ben and my grandpa Derek had been teaching combat skills to some of the newer GASP members. It had been quiet in The Shade of late, and all three men had decided it was the perfect time to hone skills and ensure that all of GASP was more than ready for whatever might lie ahead.

"Good," Tejus replied. "Field and his brothers are

impressive. They don't over-rely on their ability to make a quick exit, which is commendable. They're all highly skilled, and quick to learn. Field in particular. He's going to make a good leader one day." He paused, softly kissing the top of my head. "Just like our child will."

I rolled my eyes. Of course our child would. With a father like Tejus, I couldn't imagine it being any other way.

"Was Benedict okay?" I asked. My brother had been desperate to join in the training for weeks now, but without having become a vampire yet because of his age, my dad and grandpa forbade it. It was too dangerous for a human.

"Not really." Tejus sighed. "He hates being left out, but there's nothing I can do... I think he also misses Yelena."

I nodded. I thought that too. Ever since she'd left, Benedict had been difficult. He completely denied it when I inquired if he missed her, but anyone could see that he did. Still, he had Julian and his other friends on the island. I hoped he would get over it soon. I also hoped that Yelena's parents would let her return in the summer, which wasn't far away.

"That reminds me," I said. "Ruby and Ash are returning soon—just to stay for a few weeks."

"What about the brownies?" Tejus smirked.

"They're staying, apparently," I replied, still slightly bemused by the way that had turned out. The brownies had been sent over to Nevertide to help with the clean-up and had actually been helpful—which had come as a surprise to everyone, especially my mother. The creatures had liked Nevertide so much that they'd requested permission to stay and build a small community of their own. Ash and Ruby had been only too happy to oblige. The brownies' stealing tendencies seemed to have been eradicated by hard labor, and now that Nevertide was up and running again, they both figured it was the more the merrier.

"Will Ruby and Ash come again for the birth?" Tejus asked.

I snorted. "Yes. Apparently, even if the bump is ready to come out, I have to hold on till Ruby gets here, or I'm in deep trouble."

"Oh, really?" Tejus replied, an acerbic tone creeping into his voice. "You can tell Ruby that if she puts undue stress on my wife during labor, *she'll* be the one in trouble."

I laughed, knowing he was only half-joking. My husband's protective instincts had ratcheted up a couple of notches since news of the pregnancy, and it looked like it would continue at maximum until I had our child.

Thinking about Ruby and Ash, who still hadn't undergone their vampire transformation, reminded me that it was something Tejus and I still hadn't decided on. I knew that it was a certainty for both of us, but I just didn't know when. If we definitely wanted another child, we'd need to wait several more years, preferably until he or she was past their toddler stage.

"What are you thinking?" Tejus asked after a pause, and I realized I'd drifted off into my own thoughts again.

"About us eventually turning into vampires." *Well, sentry-vamps.*

"I've been thinking about that too," he said. "I do think we should delay it, in case we want another."

I smiled. "Another bump."

"Exactly," he confirmed.

I let out a contented sigh. "In any case, when we do eventually turn, we'll have to do it in shifts, so both of us aren't consumed by hunger at the same time."

Tejus bent further down, gently twisting me sideways so that I faced him. His eyes were dark and hooded, sending shivers running down my spine. His lips pressed against mine, his kiss drawing the breath out of me. I snaked my arms up and around his shoulders, my heart palpitating furiously as my husband held me against him.

"Hazel, when you're around, I'm always consumed by hunger."

HAZEL

"Where's Corrine?" Grace asked, after she'd said hello to Victoria and me. We were waiting for the witch in the Sanctuary, enjoying cups of herbal tea that Corrine had delivered before rushing off to attend to my brother.

"She'll be in soon. She's just finishing up with Benedict. He's managed to scrape both his arms trying to climb one of the redwoods." I sighed. Poor Benedict. It was a good thing that he was out and about more since we'd returned from Nevertide, rather than pining for a game console, but I wished he'd stop taking such stupid risks.

"Nothing serious though?" Grace asked.

"No." I shook my head. "Nothing serious. How are *you* feeling?"

Grace laughed. "Well, hungry pretty much twenty-four-seven, and sleepy…you?" She looked at Victoria and me expectantly.

"Exactly the same," Victoria replied, rubbing her belly. "My little half-cub is really kicking up a storm at the moment."

"Can I feel?" I asked.

"Go ahead," Victoria replied, leaning further back in her chair. "Does anyone mind if I take a short nap?"

We both smiled knowingly. Sleep was a major luxury for us at the moment. I placed a hand over her stomach, feeling the child's movements against her skin. It *was* active.

The door to the room in the Sanctuary opened, and we all turned, expecting Corrine to walk through, but it was Vivienne, my mom, and my grandma Sofia, grinning broadly at the three of us.

"How are we all doing?" my mom asked.

"Not quite beached whales yet, but it won't be long," I muttered. She smirked, and the women took a seat. "Especially me."

By far my stomach was the largest of the three of us. Of

course it was. With a sentry husband, I couldn't have expected anything different.

"It's certainly impressive," my grandma replied, grinning with the happiness of someone who didn't need to actually carry around the humongous child.

Grace's bump was the smallest. She was convinced it was a girl, that she could feel the energy of her child and that it was definitely feminine.

"Have you and Tejus tried to mind-meld with your baby yet?" Grace asked me.

I shook my head. "We did think about it, but it's probably too early, and we're worried we might accidentally syphon off it when we make contact. It just feels risky. Neither of us knows enough about the syphoning process to be sure that it won't affect the baby negatively."

"I think that's a good idea," Vivienne agreed.

Corrine swept in, smiling brightly at us all. We had all been having regular check-ups in the Sanctuary, just so that Corrine could make sure we were all on track. She was being extra-cautious in monitoring us since we had all gotten pregnant at around the same time. As a result, Corrine wanted to make absolutely sure that she wasn't missing anything, getting to know the development of our children as well as she could before we gave birth. If all three came at once, she wanted to be as prepared as possible.

"You're all here, good! Rose, I've sent Benedict home, he's fine. Just a few grazes, nothing I couldn't fix."

"Thanks, Corrine," my mom said, sighing.

"So, on to you." Corrine smiled down at me, placing her hands on my stomach. She left them there for a while, nodding happily.

"All good here," she confirmed, and then moved to do the same to Victoria and Grace. She gave the same murmurs of satisfaction at examining both of them, and then turned to face us all, her eyes bright. "I can actually tell you the gender of your children…if you want to know?"

Vivienne, my mom and grandma looked at us excitedly.

"Yes," I replied. "I do. Vicky, Grace?" I turned to the others.

"I'm positive mine's a girl, but yes," Grace confirmed.

Victoria took longer to make up her mind, glancing thoughtfully at her mother. "I don't think I will," she replied eventually. "I want it to be a surprise."

"Of course!" Corrine exclaimed, winking at Victoria. "It's a secret I'll keep to myself then."

"So, is mine a girl?" Grace asked. Corrine nodded. Grace

looked down at her stomach, a smile playing on her lips as she protectively ran a hand across her bump. Her cheeks flushed a delicate pink in gratitude and I felt my eyes well up. It was such a lovely moment—I couldn't wait for Grace's girl to be born. No doubt she would be just as beautiful and graceful as her mother was.

"And you, Hazel, you're having a boy!" Corrine delivered the news with rapture.

I laughed. It didn't come as a surprise, judging by my size. The baby inside me was all Tejus, and I couldn't wait for him to enter the world.

"Oh, I can't believe it!" my mom burst out, tears running down her cheeks as she hurriedly tried to wipe them away. "I can't believe you're having a baby boy, Hazel! And I'm going to be a grandmother…your father's going to be *so* excited."

We all hugged and congratulated one another, my grandma looking dizzy with amazement as she came to grips with the idea of being a great-grandmother to the new arrivals.

"I love to see The Shade expanding." My grandma sighed happily. "Derek and I wished for nothing more. And even now, it hardly seems real…I never could have guessed how much happiness I had in store for me. I've been well and truly blessed."

I glanced over at Grace and Victoria. Since we'd first heard the news of our simultaneous pregnancies, we had wondered if the Oracle had something to do with it. On the day of the wedding I had dismissed the Oracle's strange action—how she had placed her hands on all three of our stomachs, and murmured something about our 'strong tribe'. But after we'd found out about our pregnancies, her actions had come back to me, and I felt that perhaps we had her to thank for the healthy children we'd been blessed with.

"What?" my grandmother asked, noticing the way I was looking at Grace and Victoria.

"It's something the Oracle did." I shrugged, explaining what had happened at my and Ruby's wedding.

"That is… odd." My grandmother looked a little worried. She paused to glance at my mother and Vivienne, wetting her lower lip. "Perhaps it was a superstition of her people."

I grimaced. Thinking about the 'people' of the Oracle didn't exactly make me feel warm and fuzzy—the Oracle had been half Ancient. *Not* a pleasant species.

"Well, if she is the reason we're all having kids at the same time," Victoria said with a shrug, "I'm not complaining. It means I have the two of you to keep me company."

Grace and I smirked. I was also thankful that I had two others to share this with. Of course, I had my mom and grandma, who knew exactly what they were talking about, but in terms of sharing the day-to-day aches, pains and sleepless nights, Grace and Victoria had been invaluable.

By the time I got this chunky sentry baby out of me, I suspected I would owe a lot of people my sanity.

Victoria

"Let me do this," Bastien scolded me, taking the wooden spoon from my hand. "You should be relaxing."

I replied by grabbing the spoon back. "I've had enough of lounging around."

It was true. For me, being active was better. It helped relax my cub's growing urges—especially around night-time. Even though half-human, half-werewolf children couldn't transform into wolves, I'd learned from having Jovi that they could still feel restless.

Bastien had started growing out his facial hair, and I gave it a playful tug. He ignored the boiling pots and pans on the stove and wrapped his arms around me.

His natural scent always grew muskier around this time of day, when he was due to turn. My hands roamed across his muscled back, sensing his increase in body temperature.

"So you really didn't want to know what it was?" he asked, referring to the check-up I'd had in the Sanctuary earlier in the day.

"I'm going to be happy either way, so I don't feel like I need to know. And Jovi's going to be pleased if it's a boy or girl. He keeps asking when it's coming, like he's waiting for a birthday present."

Bastien laughed. "I know. He's looking forward to having someone to play with. Personally though, I sense it's a girl."

"You do?" I asked in surprise. He hadn't shared that theory with me before, and I kept changing my mind, one moment positive it was a girl, the next one hundred percent certain it was a boy.

"I do." He nodded, running a hand down my back. "And she's going to be just as incredible as her mother."

My spine tingled as he drew closer and began to press slow kisses down my neck. I groaned softly, my arms draping over his shoulders.

"You're teasing me too much, Bastien," I breathed.

Gently he moved away, his hands resting on my hips. "I'm sorry," he replied huskily. "I can't help myself. Especially when your body looks like this."

I rolled my eyes, laughing. My body had changed a lot— my usually slim frame had become more curvaceous, especially in the chest area. Thank goodness for Corrine and her seamstress skills.

I was about to reply when a knock came from the front door. "I'll get it," I said. "You finish up in here."

I slipped away from Bastien and made my way to the door, greeting Micah, Kira, Saira and five other werewolves we'd invited for dinner, before they all went out for a run around the island together (an exercise routine some of the wolves had adopted recently). They piled into the kitchen, their eyes bulging in appreciation as they smelled the food.

"Leave some for my wife!" Bastien warned playfully as the pack descended on the food we'd laid out on the table.

I called for Jovi and he came toddling in from where he'd been playing in the living room, saying 'hullo' to the bump, as he did about three times a day. We all sat and ate around the table, our guests thoroughly enjoying themselves until their transformation time approached.

Then they piled out of the door, leaving just Bastien, our son and me.

"Don't you dare clean up," Bastien said. "I'll do it when I get back."

"I clean!" Jovi volunteered.

Bastien stooped to kiss our son's rosy cheeks. "Thank you for offering, Jovi—that's kind of you. But you know it's your bath time now."

Jovi was still far too young to actually help, though that didn't stop him from trying…he would just sweetly make more mess until he felt he'd 'finished' the task.

"I'll see you later," I said, kissing my husband goodbye.

As our lips parted, instead of drawing away to leave, Bastien clutched my arms and held me closer. "Victoria," he whispered in my ear, "I hope you're prepared to make an entire pack with me."

I burst out laughing before pushing him toward the door, half horrified and half delighted at the thought of more pregnancies.

"Go on!" I exclaimed. "Just run it out!"

He winked at me. "I'll be back before you know it."

I shut the door, still smiling to myself.

"Your father's insane," I told Jovi, before realizing the

boy had slid out of his chair, leaving a trail of food smudges across the kitchen floor that led into the living room… where he would be hiding under the sofa to escape bath time.

River

I sat next to my daughter Grace, both of us looking out across The Shade, enjoying the still silence of the day coming to an end. Lawrence and Field would be arriving soon, back from training, and I wanted to be here when she told her husband the news of their baby girl. I still couldn't believe that my daughter was starting her own family, but I supposed that was the way I'd felt at her wedding too. I was always stunned at how fast she had grown up—I wanted to hold on to every precious moment so that it lasted an eternity. I'd missed so much with Field as he'd grown up in the harpy orphanage, and I wanted to make sure that with

Grace I paid particular attention to every passing moment, and no doubt I'd want to do the same when it came to her baby girl.

"I can hear them," Grace murmured. I nodded. So could I. They were obviously still practicing their moves. I heard a thump and a grunt as Lawrence was thrown down by Field, and both Grace and I laughed. According to Tejus and Ben, Field was showing his true colors—a born warrior who would do the whole island proud. He already made me as proud as he possibly could, warrior or not.

"Hey, Mom," Field announced in greeting as he arrived on the terrace. "What's going on?"

I grinned. "Grace has some good news."

Field's face lit up, and Lawrence appeared behind him, his eyes fixed on his wife.

"Did you find out?" he asked, a broad smile breaking across his handsome features.

Grace nodded, jumping up into his arms. "We're having a girl!"

Lawrence swung her around, and as he did so, I caught a glimpse of his expression. He looked so elated, a fierce pride in his brown eyes as he clasped my daughter to him, looking like he never wanted to let her go. He had been so looking forward to the birth—building a wooden crib and preparing the baby room.

"Congratulations, Grace." Field grinned. "Both of you. I'm looking forward to being an uncle. Does Dad know yet?" he asked, turning to me.

I shook my head; we'd be telling Ben tonight. My heart was already swelling at the thought of my husband's reaction.

I glanced back at the couple, nudging Field in the direction of home. It looked like we should give my daughter and her husband some alone time. Field smirked, and flew down from the treehouse.

Grace extracted herself from Lawrence and flung her arms around me. "I want to be the one to tell Dad. Can you all come round a bit later?"

"Of course, sweetheart." She let go of me and I waved goodbye to Lawrence, then joined Field on the ground below.

"Have you got anything going on tonight?" I asked, not knowing if he would be joining me and Ben this evening. Field spent most of his time with his brothers or Maura, his girlfriend, and it was a rare occasion when we got him for the entire evening.

"Nope," he replied, flinging an arm around my shoulder. "No plans tonight. Thought I'd hang around with you and Dad, if that's okay?"

"Of course," I scolded, leaning up to peck him on the cheek. "I always want you with us, Field. Our home is your home—a fact you seem to forget a lot of the time."

"I don't forget," he replied. "It's just still a bit weird having an actual *home*. No matter how many years it's been, I still can't quite get used to the idea." He shrugged. "And you know I prefer sleeping outdoors anyway."

"I know." I smiled. "Weirdo."

"I know, I know." He shrugged.

"What about when you move in with Maura, what are you going to do then?" I asked. He spent so much of his time there, I often wondered why it hadn't happened already, but I supposed there was no real rush.

"I don't know," he replied, his expression shedding the lightheartedness of a moment ago and becoming pensive.

"Have you settled on any, um, longer-term plans?" I enquired gently.

Field went quiet. I wondered if I'd put my foot in it somehow, but a moment later he began to reply, his voice hesitant.

26

"I'm not sure," he said slowly. "Sometimes I don't know if Maura and I are…forever, you know?"

His comment surprised me. They had been dating for a long time, and I'd hoped that Field had found the same happiness that Ben and I shared. I tried not to let my surprise show, but I was silent for just a second too long.

"I mean, we're happy together," he added. "I suppose I just wonder how you *know* that it's forever—like how you and Dad knew? Or Grace and Lawrence. I sometimes think that I'm just missing that part of me…that part that can totally trust my instincts. I keep thinking that I should ask Maura to marry me, but then something stops me—I don't know what. It's not like I don't love her, or care for her deeply."

I looked over at my son—at his aquamarine-colored eyes, dulled by worry, and the frown that marred his brow. After growing up without parents or a home, after the trauma he'd endured in the harpy "orphanage", once Field arrived in The Shade to live with us, I'd hoped he'd never experience true anxiety again. That, at least so far as his personal life went, it would be smooth and easy from then on. Of course, I knew that was unrealistic, but seeing him troubled always made me ache inside.

"With your father and me," I said, my speech slowing as I tried to give my reply consideration, "it was easy. I knew in every bone in my body that he was the one for me. I knew that early on in our relationship. But it's not always like that. Sometimes love grows slowly, it takes longer to assert itself—for both people to realize they're in love. Either way it's just as meaningful. And you might not be ready yet to settle down and start a family, but that's fine. It needs to be in your own time, honey."

He nodded, digesting my words. A span of silence passed, and then he seemed to shift out of his reverie.

"You're right," he said, glancing down at me. "Maybe one day Maura and I will think about marriage. Maybe neither of us are ready yet. I haven't even asked Maura how she might feel about that… It's never really come up."

I nodded. "You need to do what you feel is right for the both of you," I replied.

We were nearly back at home, and our conversation returned to Grace and their new baby girl. I kept the rest of my thoughts on Field and Maura to myself. I knew that my son loved her, and went out of his way to be there for her. He was kind, loving and considerate. They had a good relationship that had brought both of them happiness, but

I wondered how long it would last. I was glad that Field had opened up to me about it—their relationship was a subject that I'd been wondering about for a while now. I just didn't want Field to have to suffer heartbreak if things didn't go as they planned…But perhaps I was worrying for nothing. Taking things slowly hadn't exactly been my experience of love, but I'd meant what I said. I knew it didn't always happen like that. Field would work it out for himself. If it was meant to be, it was meant to be.

Only time would tell…

SOFIA
EIGHTEEN YEARS LATER...

I had thought I was alone in the Sanctuary's courtyard, but a rustle in the nearby bushes announced the arrival of Lucifer, Tejus and Hazel's haughty lynx. He purred around my ankles, a far friendlier creature than had arrived here... over eighteen years ago now.

Where has the time gone?

I reached down and petted the feline's soft fur, jumping slightly as he dashed off again—no doubt to hunt down some poor, helpless prey in the forest... or get himself found by Shadow the dog.

I straightened, my eyes returning to the peaceful scene that surrounded me. I resumed my silent walk among the moon-dappled gravestones, the dewy grass crunching beneath my feet, the gentle breeze carrying the warm scent of the redwoods, until I arrived at my destination—the old stone fountain at the center. I gazed down upon the two gravestones in front of it, where two of the dearest friends I'd ever had were laid to rest. I shifted the two bouquets of white roses I carried in one arm and laid them across each of the stones, careful not to cover their engraved names... *Anna and Kyle.*

It had been two years since we'd lost Anna, three since we'd lost Kyle, to the one thing no amount of jinni or witch magic could stop: time.

Like me, Anna had been an immune, which meant she couldn't turn into a vampire like a normal human. Unlike me, she'd never been 'cured' of her immunity. It was sobering to think that, if I hadn't been kidnapped to Cruor all those years ago, I never would have lost my immunity either. I would have lived a mortal life, and probably be lying here with them in this courtyard.

We'd considered more than once taking Anna to Cruor to see if its atmosphere broke her immunity, like it had done mine. Anna and Kyle's children—Jason, Ariana, and young Kiev (who were all vampires and, like my descendants, thankfully hadn't had the immunity passed on to them)—had eventually convinced Anna to visit Cruor, now that the threat of the Elders had died down and they'd become almost nonexistent shadows. But Anna's immunity wouldn't break—the intensity of the Elders' former power no longer infused the atmosphere. My son Ben, who knew more about Cruor than most of us thanks to the unfortunate time he'd spent there, had escorted her and Kyle there… only to return with the discovery that Anna still couldn't turn.

The revelation didn't come as a blow to Anna, who had already resigned herself to live a mortal life, and neither did it to Kyle, who had sworn to live out his human life alongside her.

To the rest of the island, however, their eventual deaths had been almost unbearable, crashing over us in waves of grief. Although they'd died natural deaths—both fully aware and at peace with their passing—Anna and Kyle were, especially to those who had lived in The Shade since the very early days, practically fixtures of the island. We'd known in the back of our minds that they wouldn't be with us forever, but when surrounded by so much immortality, so much power and magic, so much *choice*, it was easy to forget what it meant for life to take its natural course. Easy to be... completely blindsided by it.

I swallowed back the lump that had formed in my throat, and took a deep breath in an attempt to still my palpitating heart. We'd had a fair amount of time to mourn our friends, but visiting their gravestones still made me choke up. I doubted that would ever change.

Though I did try to remind myself that we hadn't truly lost them. That, wherever souls who passed in peace did go after death, somehow in spirit they were still with us... And they would live on through their children. Their three brave, beautiful children, whose features reminded me of their incredible parents every time I looked at them.

I took a few more minutes to compose myself before stepping back, my eyes leaving the gravestones. I continued on my walk around the courtyard, though I still remained lost in memories and contemplation.

So much in The Shade had grown and prospered in the time that had passed.

Tejus and Hazel had undergone their vampiric transformation (as had Ruby and Ash, who still lived in

Nevertide)—and Derek and I had great-grandchildren. Our great-grandson, Phoenix Hellswan, was now eighteen years old, and similar to his father Tejus in almost every way. I loved him deeply, had been grateful for every second of watching him grow into a young man—from the fat bouncing baby phase that his mother and I felt was far too short, to the imperious years of being a toddler, making demands like a little prince, and then to the moody early-to-mid teen years (his father and mother had both been relieved when those were over), to now—a handsome, intelligent and fierce warrior with integrity in bucket loads.

We also had two great-granddaughters.

Vita Conway, born to Grace and Lawrence, was the same age as Phoenix. She was a beautiful, semi-fae girl with brilliant turquoise eyes and gold-brown hair, and her face looked so much like her mother that over the years it was becoming harder to tell the two apart. Vita was shy and quiet, intent on developing her inherent fae abilities. Fascinated by nature and the cosmos, both she and Zerus, Tejus's brother, spent many hours trying to decipher messages and order in the night's sky. I knew she would grow to become an amazing member of GASP—even more so when she broke free of her shy reserve.

I smiled to myself as I thought of my other great-granddaughter. She certainly had no issues with reserve. Serena Hellswan, Hazel and Tejus's second child, was the polar opposite of Vita. Serena was a firecracker—a ball of energy and determination who ran around without ever letting up. Ever since she was a child she'd found it impossible to sit still, wanting to walk long before she could crawl, and so early to talk that it had shocked everyone. Tejus and Phoenix had their work cut out for them. Serena had the most protective father and brother in the world, and she constantly fought to carve out her own independence, determined that she didn't need the constant guardianship of either of them. It was only the profound love that their family shared which stopped epic fights from erupting— and the presence of Hazel, who was always mediator, acting as a buffer against Tejus and Phoenix's protective instincts. I knew that one day Serena would be glad of both her father and brother's desire to keep her sheltered, but at seventeen, she wanted her freedom—and was determined to get it.

Serena Hellswan, Vita Conway and Aida Blackhall—the half-werewolf daughter of Victoria and Bastien—had struck up a firm friendship. Though Serena was a year younger than Aida and Vita, it never seemed to matter. The girls were as thick as thieves, their escapades as children legendary. Together, with Serena as the most likely ringleader, they had caused more mischief in The Shade than a bunch of brownies. Still, that was in the past. Now well on their way to adulthood, the girls were maturing, slowly becoming the exceptional women I knew they would be.

We also had another addition to The Shade. Yelena, Benedict's childhood friend, had visited us every summer since her return from Nevertide, right up until she was sixteen. She had stopped coming then, sending Benedict a letter telling him that she had a boyfriend now, and would be moving to New York to finish her final years of school. Benedict had told everyone that he didn't mind—that he was glad she wouldn't be coming to 'bother' him every summer. That had lasted for two years while his mother and I waited patiently for him to see sense. Two years later, just after his eighteenth birthday, Benedict had started to grow restless. He packed his bags, left his mom a note that he'd gone in search of her, and disappeared from The Shade.

He was back a month later. He wouldn't speak a word to us about what had happened, and refused to even talk to Hazel or Rose about whether or not he'd found her. It was two months after his return that Yelena called Corrine's phone and arrived at Benedict's door, bags in hand. The couple hadn't parted since, and were now both vampires— and married, with a twelve-year-old daughter. I never found out what happened when he went looking for Yelena, and perhaps I'd never know… but as long as they remained happy together, I was thrilled.

The Hawk boys had also seen change, or the absence of it. At around twenty years old (it was difficult to determine their exact age), their half-blood vampire genes had kicked in. They had stopped visibly aging and appeared frozen like regular vampires, which came as a surprise to all of us. We'd thought they would continue to age like regular humans, but years had passed now, and Field and his brothers had remained unchanged. Field and Maura had had a lot of ups and downs in their relationship in the time that had gone by—a lot of breaking up and getting back together again, and they still weren't married. At this point, I wasn't sure what the eventual outcome would be—I just hoped that soon enough they'd figure out what they both wanted for themselves, and settle down… with or without each other.

Maura's brother Orlando, on the other hand, had married seventeen years ago. He tied the knot with his love

Regan, the half-human, half-dragon twenty-year-old daughter of Azaiah. It had taken Azaiah a long time to come to terms with Orlando and Regan's coupling (and a lot of *heated* discussions), since he'd always hoped she would marry a fire dragon. Regan was one of the few dragon hybrids on the island who was able to shift into a beastly form, in spite of her mixed blood, and would have been invaluable to the fire dragon race as a whole in helping to populate The Hearthlands. Azaiah had no choice but to give his blessing in the end, considering his daughter's happiness was on the line, and now Orlando and Regan had two beautiful daughters—seventeen-year-old Saskia, and sixteen-year-old Opal.

Jeramiah Novak and his wife Pippa Hendry-Novak, also had a daughter—eighteen-year-old Scarlett. There was a period after she was born when Derek had found no end of fun in calling Lucas "Gramps" every time they saw each other around the island. I supposed my husband had been waiting a long time to get his own back, since Lucas hadn't exactly been sparing with the term when our first grandchild, Grace, was born. There were times when you could tell from the dazed look on Lucas's face that he couldn't quite believe the situation he'd ended up in, a family man—a family that would only keep expanding—but I had to admit, my brother-in-law had stepped up to the role admirably well... He was almost behaving like an adult. His adopted daughter Avril was also grown up now, which made him a fatherly figure to two young women.

On the whole, we had experienced an incredible amount of peace over the past eighteen years. The last big supernatural warfare was Nevertide, and since then only a few, minor incidents had occurred. The most memorable was the strange swamp monsters in the Bayou which we had eventually managed to remove. Taking them back to The Shade had not been an option, but eventually we'd found them a home in a nature reserve, where they spent their days munching on litter. According to the local Parks and Recreation team, their services were invaluable. We'd also had to deal with a newly formed clan of rogue vampires causing trouble in Kansas, but a GASP team, headed by Derek, Ben and Tejus, had managed to deal with that problem quickly and effectively.

Each day of peace made me more and more proud of what we'd managed to accomplish with GASP—we were now living in a time where supernaturals and humans could co-exist almost in harmony.

I started to make my way back toward the training ground. Derek would be finished there soon, and we could wander home together. These times of peace were blissful, not just because it meant that GASP's ambitions were being fulfilled, but also because it meant that my husband and I could actually spend more time together—a calm, tranquil existence that we'd always dreamed of. A true sanctuary.

In two days' time, we'd be making a trip to the In-Between. Queen Nuriya and Sherus had given birth to a baby boy, or more correctly, a baby fae-jinn—the first of its kind, as far as I knew. We would be traveling to the fire faes' abode for a child 'welcoming' ritual, popular with the fae. Everyone from The Shade who wanted to come had been invited, and the children and young adults had talked of little else in the past few weeks.

The jinni queen and the fae king had been wed for a while now. After Nevertide the two of them had spent more and more time together—Sherus had determinedly set out to woo Nuriya with his sister's help. I laughed to myself. To onlookers, the queen had appeared impervious to his charms, but he had eventually worn her down, and not a soul now doubted that the jinni queen was just as much in love with her husband as he was with her. As I walked along,

I wondered what a child of two such powerful species would be like—it would be gifted with so many abilities, so much inherent potential…

"Sofia?" Derek called my name, and I turned to see him jogging up the path to meet me, his dark hair scattered over his forehead. I waited for him to arrive, grinning as he took my hand in his and clasped it firmly at his side.

"How was your day?" I asked, brushing hair away from his brilliant blue eyes.

"Much improved now." He smiled boyishly down at me. I didn't know how his gaze could still set me on fire the way it did. After so many years, one would have thought that my all-consuming love of Derek would have died a little, but if anything, it was the opposite—it just grew deeper, stronger, and so filled with respect and honesty that it felt like he had become the other half of my physical being, that I just wouldn't make sense without him. "Yours?" he asked.

"Filled with memories… I went to pay my respects to Anna and Kyle."

"Ah." He nodded, his Adam's apple bobbing as he swallowed. He let go of my hand, and I felt his chest tighten as he drew me closer in an embrace.

We stood like that for a while, holding each other, our

eyes closed, relishing the bewitching tranquility of our island: the chirping of the birds above us, the occasional burst of laughter or shout of someone's name in the distance, the crashing of the waves against the shore.

Then, without saying a word, Derek and I drew apart and walked in the direction of the lighthouse.

When we arrived on the beach where the structure stood tall and proud, after so many centuries of struggle and battles, the sight of it stirred up so many memories in me. I glanced over at Derek's noble profile in the light of the moon. With all the changes that The Shade had undergone—the lives progressing, the ups and downs of day-to-day existence—it struck me that through all of it, the love between Derek and me had been the one constant… In a way, it was what The Shade had been founded on.

"I love you," I whispered, as we neared the rocks.

Derek stopped walking, his electric-blue eyes filling with emotion as they settled on me. He cupped my face before leaning in to gently kiss my lips. His voice was husky as he replied, "And I love you, Sofia."

Aida
[Victoria and Bastien's daughter]

I flew through the air, landing on the hard, dusty ground of the training area with a thump. *Man*, my butt hurt. Phoenix stood a couple of feet away, smirking.

"Nice," I retorted grumpily as I clambered to my feet and rubbed my behind.

"You told me not to hold back," he reminded me.

I regret that.

"Yeah, yeah," I mumbled, pulling myself together, ready to aim my own blow. With a grunt, I launched myself at him. My left leg swerved behind him as my arm shot out to palm-hit him in the chest. He stumbled, but was too quick—he jumped back over my leg rather than falling, and took up his attack stance again.

"Dammit," I exhaled, breathing hard.

"What's with you today?" he asked, laughing.

"Feeling a little low on energy," I replied, eyeing him suspiciously. "Know why that might be?"

Phoenix shook his head, his lips molding into a smirk. "If you think I'm cheating, guess again—you're just off your game."

I raised a questioning brow, not quite trusting that the sentry wasn't using his syphoning powers to drain me. That was the problem with fighting with Phoenix. He always swore he wasn't cheating, but sometimes I wasn't sure.

"Whatever..." I grinned suddenly, giving him the benefit of the doubt. Phoenix's syphoning abilities weren't subtle – I was sure I would have been able to tell if he had. This time he launched forward, but I managed to swerve out of the way. My shoulder was knocked sideways, but I kept my ground.

"Better," he intoned, spinning into a back kick. It landed on my already painful backside, sending me flying forward. My glutes seized up, and I swore under my breath.

"How are you so damn perky this morning anyway?" I asked, more angrily than I intended. I would have some serious bruising tonight. "Serena told me you got back at the crack of dawn this morning...another trip to Hawaii?"

Phoenix's brow furrowed and it was my turn to smirk.

"My sister should learn discretion," he growled, flying at me again. We fought hand to hand, punches hitting their marks with hollow thuds, till Phoenix landed a well-aimed punch to my right side and I staggered backward.

"Who was the girl this time?" I replied, laughing at his annoyance. I loved winding Phoenix up—sometimes it was just too easy, especially when I had the inside scoop from his younger sister.

This time though, Phoenix just laughed.

"None of your business," he replied, sending another kick my way. He was fast this morning—yesterday's date had obviously gone well. I'd forgotten that Phoenix seemed to thrive on his trips outside The Shade, no doubt syphoning at will and sweeping another poor, unsuspecting damsel off her feet.

"Oh, Phoenix," I cooed, "you're so handsome—I wish my hair was as nice as yours." I fluttered my lashes dramatically, playing the part of the love-sick crushes I imagined he picked up in the human world.

He boomed with laughter, grabbing me around the waist to try to knock me down on the floor. I was too quick for him this time, slithering out of his grasp and shoving him backward. He didn't fall, but was still bent over laughing.

My amusement dried up quickly as I saw Field standing at the edge of the clearing, watching us. His arms were folded across his chest, a white t-shirt showing off his toned biceps and highlighting his dark features. I blushed under his speculative gaze.

I'd totally forgotten about Phoenix, so when his attack came, I was completely defenseless. Once again, I went flying across the training yard from the force of Phoenix's full body-slam, my back smacking into the ground and skidding to a halt.

I lay still, looking up at the dark sky and trying to catch my breath.

Humiliating.

"Watch yourself, cub." Field's voice drifted over, and then his head appeared over mine, blocking out the sky. His lips were turned up in a small smile, a dimple appearing on his right cheek.

Without saying a word, I scrambled to my feet, inwardly

begging myself to cool my blushes. I dusted off my training uniform without looking up.

"Hey, Field," I muttered.

Phoenix's footsteps crunched on the gravel as he came over to join us. He was trying his best not to laugh.

"Are you all right?" he asked me, his concern somehow making it worse.

"I'm fine," I replied quickly, "glad to be put through my paces."

"Liar," he replied, slinging his arm around my shoulders in a half-hearted apology while turning his attention to Field. "Want to have a go? I'm warning you, I'm feeling pretty spry." Phoenix cracked his neck from side to side, grinning with all the cockiness of someone who had just landed his opponent on the ground.

"It's so tempting," Field replied. "Someone's got to knock you down, but it can't be me today—I'm on my way to see Maura. Tomorrow?"

Phoenix nodded. "Challenge accepted."

At the mention of Maura, I started to back away, leaving them to discuss their training session. My boots scraped at the ground in frustration.

What is wrong with me?

I mentally kicked myself for not appearing more composed in front of Field. It just wasn't okay to behave that way—partly because it made me look like a total idiot, and partly because he was with Maura. I needed to get over my stupid crush and get that into my head. I couldn't compete with his girlfriend, and I didn't even want to try: I really, *really* didn't want to be that kind of girl, swooning after someone else's boyfriend.

Maybe I'd be a bit more satisfied if I had Maura's composure, her normal human looks…and her lack of *hair*. I wasn't bad now, but growing up… Ugh. Thanks to my father's wolf genes, my hair had been out of control. It had just grown everywhere, like an unstoppable curse that chipped away at my self-esteem from early puberty till I was about fifteen. That was when I'd begged Corrine to intervene. After a short episode of pleading, the witch had saved the day. She'd created a potion—not the nicest-tasting stuff, but who cared?—and after taking it every day for six months, my hair problem had disappeared, leaving it only in the places it should be. Things were *so* much better now, though I still sometimes acted like I was covered in hair. Like if I ever stood in direct sunlight—luckily not such a huge problem when we were in The Shade—I worried that everyone could see nonexistent fuzz on my face.

It was all right for my older brother, Jovi. He was hairy, but it just looked cool on him, mainly making him appear older and more dark and brooding than he actually was.

Field and Phoenix looked like they were finishing off their conversation, and I prepared myself for another ass-kicking. I watched the two men as they said goodbye—they were kind of similar in many ways, both dark-haired and muscular, with dark stubble covering their jaws, but Phoenix always appeared more arrogant and proud because he'd inherited Tejus's distinct features. Though Field's face was just as chiseled and stark, there was something gentler about his appearance. I supposed he was more traditionally handsome than Phoenix, and the dimple that appeared on his cheek when he smiled… *that* drove me to distraction.

Field waved in my direction before heading off, and I returned it, smiling as brightly as I could. He leapt into the sky, those dark dagger wings of his expanding so that he looked like some deadly avenging angel, before he shot up into the air and disappeared from sight.

"Oh, Field," cooed Phoenix, "you're so handsome—fly away with me?"

"Shut up," I hissed, "he'll hear you!"

"He's gone." Phoenix shrugged. "But your face could still fry a pancake. If you're so into him, why don't you just talk to him?"

"I'm *not* into him," I replied, biting my bottom lip in annoyance.

"Sure," Phoenix drawled. "Totally immune to the charms of Field. Got it."

Enough talking.

I flew at Phoenix, pre-empting his flying kick by grabbing onto his boot and spinning him over. The moment he tried to land, I knocked his back leg from under him and sent him sprawling across the training ground.

Finally.

"Still feeling spry?" I asked with a grin.

SERENA
[HAZEL AND TEJUS'S DAUGHTER]

I flicked through the campus website tabs on my laptop. There were so many to choose from, but browsing was more of an indulgence than an actual exercise in choice. I already knew that I wanted to study English at Brown, but as Corrine repeatedly reminded me, it wouldn't do any harm to broaden my search. Today I wanted to check the tour schedules. If I was going to get Mom and Dad to take this seriously, I would need facts and dates—not just vague concepts that I'd hedged around before.

I knew Mom would be all for it, but that Dad would be

harder to work around. He didn't like the idea of me leaving The Shade, and with college being a year away, if I was going to get into any of them, I needed to start planning seriously. Education in The Shade wasn't strictly curricular, but I knew that universities tried to get a diverse range of students in, and you didn't get much more diverse than me...I didn't imagine that they'd have any applicants with the extra-curricular activities I had on their résumé.

I jotted down some of the tour dates, making sure that the Brown ones were at the top of the list. Even if I couldn't win Dad's approval, there wasn't much he could say about me visiting a campus for a day—especially not if Corrine and Mom went with me.

My parents were laughing in the kitchen. I'd specifically chosen a moment when my older brother, Phoenix, would be out of the house. I'd begged Aida to keep him busy for as long as possible, and so far, it looked like my plan was working.

"Mom, Dad?" I peered around the kitchen door, finding them both playing an old-fashioned board game that they'd originally bought for my brother. Downtime from GASP duties sure made my parents creative at ways to entertain themselves.

"There you are!" my mom exclaimed. "Do you want to play? I'm beating your father, and he's not liking it."

I looked unenthusiastically at the board game.

"I'll pass," I replied. "There's actually something I wanted to talk to you about."

My voice had come out a bit too squeaky, and my dad's eyes narrowed.

"I know that voice—what do you want?" he replied.

"That's not fair!" I said immediately. "I really did just want to talk to you both."

Dad leaned back in his chair, arms crossed, and eyed me warily. My mom rose from the table, shooting Dad a meaningful look, and smiled brightly at me.

"We're listening," she replied.

"Good," I replied, suddenly all business. The way forward was getting Mom on my side, and then she could reason with Dad. "So I've been thinking more about applying to universities, and there are a couple of open days that I'd like to attend, just to get a feel for the different campuses and see what—"

"Where are these universities?" my dad asked quickly.

"Tejus," my mom interjected. "Let her speak."

"All over North America, Dad, you know that. And you

know that I want to study the traditional way, but I just can't here."

My dad nodded silently, but his brows were still furrowed.

"I think it's a good idea," my mom replied, pursing her lips at Dad. "I'm glad that you're taking your education seriously, and we *both* want the best for you—let's have a look at the dates."

I handed her my notepad in relief. As I'd hoped, Mom was on my side. It would just be a matter of getting Dad there too.

"Dad, please can you be reasonable about this?" I pleaded.

"I am being reasonable about this," he retorted. "I want you to have everything, and a good education is part of that, but you know how dangerous the world can be. I'm not sure I want you at such a distance from your mother and me—and the protection of The Shade for that matter."

"There haven't been any problems for ages, and even those were minor," I argued.

"Rogue vampires are not minor," he replied, referring to the problems in Kansas. "Lives were lost—parents left without their children."

"I know that, Dad, but I can handle myself. If I was to live on campus, I would know exactly who to call in an emergency. It's not like distance matters that much, the witches can reach me in a matter of moments. I really don't see what the big deal is. You'd let Phoenix go!"

"I would have the same concerns if it were Phoenix asking," Dad replied. I didn't believe that for a second. Phoenix snuck out frequently to visit the mainland, getting up to God knew what in Hawaii…and all I was asking for was to go to school.

"Tejus," my mom chided softly, "give her a chance. We can at least go and visit these places. You're being over-protective, but she'll be eighteen when she attends. An adult in her own right."

My dad raked his hand through his hair, his jaw clenching. I tried to hide a gleeful smile—I knew that look. It meant Mom and I had won.

"You're right," he sighed. "But Serena, you're always going to be our little girl. Things like this are a big deal for your mother and me. We're used to knowing that wherever you are, you're safe and secure. Once you're out of The Shade, we're going to worry."

I smiled, walking over to give him a hug. I loved my

parents to pieces and I knew Dad was always over-protective. He couldn't help it—it was just the way he was, especially when it came to Mom and me.

"I know you're going to worry," I replied. "But trust me, there will be nothing to worry about. The worst thing I'll face is the mountain of homework and some human guy hitting on me during orientation."

My dad grimaced. "I'm not worried about boys—I know you can handle yourself against humans. My concerns are strictly supernatural."

"What concerns?" Phoenix strolled into the kitchen, covered in sweat and dust.

Ugh. Bad timing.

"We're discussing open days at some of the universities that Serena wants to attend," my mom informed him.

"Mom!" I groaned, knowing that I would have to fight another battle—my brother, only a year older, was just as bad as my dad.

"What?" Phoenix ignored me, looking directly at Dad. "Do you think she should leave The Shade?"

"Like you do every night?" I snapped at him.

"I'm older than you—and I'm a guy."

"What?! So?" I exclaimed. "I hope Aida handed you your

ass today."

I just didn't get it. My brother was totally awesome almost one hundred percent of the time, until it came to protecting me. He suddenly turned into a fuddy-duddy, almost worse than Dad.

"I have to agree with Serena," my mom retorted, frowning at Phoenix. "That's not how we raised you, and you know it."

"All right, I'm sorry," my brother replied, holding his hands up in a mock-guilty pose, but not looking the slightest bit sorry. "Maybe we should just think about providing her with supernatural bodyguards."

"That's not a bad idea," my dad mused.

"Are you *kidding*?" I exclaimed. This conversation was fast descending into madness. Thankfully, my mom burst out into peals of laughter.

"Absolutely not," she replied once she'd calmed down. "Both of you are out of your minds. Serena's a capable young woman, and if she wants to go to college, she's going to go to college. I'll get these dates in the calendar and see if Corrine wouldn't mind taking us."

"All right," my dad growled, smiling at my mom with barely concealed admiration.

"And for that comment," my mom continued, trying to glare at Phoenix but failing miserably, "you're going to help me make dinner."

"Happily," Phoenix replied with a smirk, taking a ridiculous floral apron off a nearby hanger and placing it over his training clothes. I snorted. If only his many admirers could see him now.

"Thanks, guys," I replied happily, glad to have gotten my way. "Aida's coming over—is it okay if I wait outside for her? Or will my life be in peril?"

"Hey, don't get too sassy," my mom replied, smacking my butt with a hand towel. I laughed, and ran out to the terrace to wait for my friend.

SERENA
[HAZEL AND TEJUS'S DAUGHTER]

Aida and I were sitting on the porch, watching the redwoods sway in the breeze. I'd been boring Aida close to death about my plans for college—she'd heard them all before anyway, but now that it was starting to look like a reality, I hadn't been able to shut up.

"I'm sorry," I groaned after a pause. "This is my thing— I know you're done talking about it."

"Hey." Aida turned to me with a frown. "That's not true. I'm genuinely happy for you, and plus, happy for myself— I'm going to be visiting constantly. Maybe sit in on a lecture or two and pick up some hot postgrad."

I laughed. "Sounds good. Please do visit. I'm excited about going, but I know I'll miss home. Obviously, I won't be telling Phoenix or Dad that, they'll just try to leverage it as an excuse not to send me."

Aida shook her head, her thick, dark-brown hair cascading down her shoulders.

"Phoenix wouldn't do that, not really. You know he's only teasing you, and sometimes…you know, he just loses his head."

"Yeah, I know." I sighed. "I should be grateful I have an older brother who cares, and doesn't just ignore me completely."

"Exactly," Aida replied. "We're both lucky in that respect."

"Yeah, but Jovi's amazing—he's never over-protective. How did you get such a laid-back brother when you're so uptight?" I joked.

"Hey! I'm not that uptight. Just self-conscious—there's a difference. And I'm not even close to Vita in that respect."

She had a point. Vita was the quietest one of us all. She was painfully shy around everyone, and probably the most gentle-natured girl I'd ever met. Both Aida and I loved her unconditionally. As quiet and shy as she was around others, when you dug beneath the surface she was the most loyal and amazing friend a girl could ever hope for.

"That's true. Where is she, anyway?" I asked, looking around as if I half-expected her to appear from the shade of the tree at any moment.

"Studying. And last I saw, getting really frustrated," Aida replied.

That was nothing new. Vita was determined to enhance her fae abilities, but she was only part fae and so her control over her powers was limited. She fervently believed that one day that would change, and I hoped for her sake it did— but until that day came, Vita was going to continue to exhaust herself trying.

"Ooh," I said, suddenly distracted, "the Hawk boys at three o'clock."

Aida whipped her head around, and we both stared down at the Hawk men strolling past. Uncharacteristically, they were walking—normally you could only catch glimpses of them up in the air, but clearly today was our lucky day.

"Don't embarrass me," Aida muttered. "Your brother did enough of that earlier."

"As if I would," I whispered back.

We watched them pass in silence. Individually they were incredibly good-looking, but when you saw them as a group together like this, the combined gene-pool took my breath away. Blue was my personal favorite—those piercing blue eyes, that muscular build and that long, windswept hair made me feel like my insides were melting. I didn't even need to glance over to know where Aida's gaze would be directed. Her crush on Field showed no signs of slowing down.

I leaned back in my chair once they'd passed.

"You know they call it a crush for a reason, right?" I asked Aida, archly.

"Yeah, I know," she replied. "I can't help it...I almost want him and Maura to hurry up and get married so that I can move on and get it out of my system once and for all. It's driving me crazy."

"Can't you focus on one of the others?" I asked. "I mean, they're all pretty easy on the eyes. Massive understatement, but you get what I mean."

"If it was just looks-based, I could." She rolled her eyes, more in irritation at herself than me. "But it's more than that. He's so kind and *honorable*, you know? Like the kind of guy who would stop and walk old ladies across the street."

I sighed, lazily stretching out so that my feet rested on the banister that surrounded the treehouse. Dad had built it when Phoenix and I were younger so we didn't fall off the terrace, but he'd never taken it down and now it had just become part of the furniture.

Through the wooden slats, I could make out Jovi standing beneath us.

"Aida, we need to get going," he called up.

Both of us leaned forward to wave.

"Coming," Aida replied.

"Hey, Serena." Jovi waved at me, flashing me a charming smile.

"Hey, Jovi." I smiled down at him. Aida's brother was another example of The Shade's ability to produce fine-looking creatures, but he was my cousin so I really couldn't see him in that way. I'd been especially close to him growing up.

"How are you?" he asked, while his sister climbed down.

"Good. Parents agreed to let me go to some college open days!" I said, sharing my good news. Jovi's smile became kind of fixed.

"You know we'd all much prefer you didn't leave us," he replied.

"Don't *you* start too," Aida interjected, nudging her brother in the chest. "She's just had her dad and brother to deal with."

He muttered something to her that I couldn't make out, before throwing her over his broad shoulders, still looking disappointed.

"It won't be forever," I replied. "What's a few years to a supernatural?"

He shrugged, shifting on his feet, before sighing. "Okay… Well, see you later I guess," he called back, starting to walk back in the direction of their home.

As I watched them disappear through the trees, I felt a slight tug at my heart. As anxious as I was to leave The Shade for study, deep down, I knew with every fiber of my being that I would miss my crazy family just as much as they missed me.

Vita
[GRACE AND LAWRENCE'S DAUGHTER]

I stared at the small flame flickering in the jar. The tea candle had almost entirely melted into runny, see-through wax. Next to the jar were six other empty candle foils—evidence of today's mounting failure.

Leaning back against the tree, I sighed in frustration. The one thing I was glad for was that there was no one around to witness my dismal attempts. I was sitting in a secluded spot by the Sanctuary, a small plot of land that Ibrahim and Corrine had kindly gifted mc to grow herbs and flowers and practice my abilities. The growing part was coming along well—the plot of land was lush with bushes of sage, feverfew, lemon balm, St. John's wort and devil's claw. I had grown them patiently, attending to them like they were small children, and reaped the rewards.

With my own abilities the opposite was true. It seemed like the more I tried, the harder it got. Sometimes, seemingly at random, my abilities would burst to the surface—an erratic breeze, or water from the tap running over onto the kitchen floor—but never in a way that was even remotely helpful, or when I wanted it to happen. Once I'd even managed to set my mom's curtain ablaze with a scented candle. She'd tried to be pleased that my abilities were surfacing, but the house just smelt burnt for about three weeks.

Refocusing, I concentrated on the near-dead candle. It fizzled, crackling, but then went out completely.

"Why won't you just work?" I groaned, taking out the dead candle and replacing it with a new one. I lit a match, and the candle spluttered to life. Placing the jar back on the ground, I held my hands over it and closed my eyes, willing the flame to rise up.

My temples started to throb from the effort, and I leaned back against the tree, wondering whether I should go and visit Serena, see if she couldn't gift me with some much-needed energy. It wouldn't be the first time she'd funneled her energy into me though a mind-meld to help me with my studies, but it was getting late.

The bushes rustled behind me, and I turned my head around to see Zerus emerging from the back door of the Sanctuary.

"Any luck today?" he asked.

I shook my head.

"Absolutely nothing. I swear I'm getting worse."

The sentry laughed and came to sit down next to me. Zerus was the only person I didn't mind being around while I practiced. I felt that, above everyone in The Shade, even my best friends, Zerus was the one who understood me best. We were both majorly introverted, and tended to keep to ourselves. Zerus, with his night-time walks and his insistence that he slept outside in the woods, was even more socially awkward than I was. I could practically see his energy draining away from him if he spoke to anyone for more than ten minutes, but it wasn't like that when it was just the two of us. We could both be ourselves, sometimes sitting in silence for hours and not saying a word.

Zerus was one of the older members of The Shade. He

had refused to become a vampire, politely declining the request, and his handsome features would continue, slowly but surely, to show signs of age.

"You're not getting worse," he corrected me, "you're getting impatient. I don't know how many times I have told you that you need to slow down, to study the natural world before you can claim ownership over it."

"Mom and Grandpa Ben don't have that problem," I pointed out.

"Grace is more fae than you are, and Benjamin certainly is. You cannot hope to match their abilities straight away—one day, perhaps, but that day is not now."

I crossed my arms, not enthused to be reminded that this would be a slower process than I'd first imagined.

Zerus laughed.

"Are you wondering what an old sentry knows about fae powers?" he asked, and my cheeks reddened. "Ah, of course you are. Don't be embarrassed. But I do know about the natural order, and I have studied the stars and the earth for a long time. What I do know is that nature never hurries—it is slow and patient. Even when we believe that something has happened in the blink of an eye, like a shooting star, nature has been building it for a time that is close to eternity for you and me."

I smiled at Zerus, loving him for his own love of nature and the world around us. I had always appreciated the way he explained things to me, just as patient and slow as he perceived nature to be. His face creased into a broad smile.

"Why not rest?" he asked gently. "Give your mind some time to recover. You are surrounded by beauty here, and yet all you do is focus on your own failure."

I looked around the garden. It *was* beautiful, but the gentle sway of lavender and the riot of colorful petals couldn't contend with the persistent tug at the back of my mind, driving me to obsess over my abilities, desperate to bring them to the surface.

"I will stop as soon as something happens to this," I proclaimed, gesturing to the candle. "I'm eighteen, Zerus, I've waited long enough."

He barked with laughter.

"Eighteen is nothing, try living to my age. You'll learn then that nothing happens in the time that it should."

"Why did you choose not to become an immortal, Zerus?" I asked, suddenly curious—I had always thought he was content with his decision, but his words made me think otherwise.

The sentry was silent for a few moments, gazing down toward the flickering flame.

"I'm afraid I am fated to be alone," he replied eventually, "and that is not something that bothers me terribly much—there are many things that bring me joy. But an immortal life alone? That is something that I couldn't bear. It is better to let my life end naturally, when it will. Perhaps," he mused, glancing up at me, "it is something that you should heed. I know you are shy and reserved, Vita, but don't let that hold you back. Not from building relationships with others. You will live a long life, make sure that it counts for something—something more than just your *own* happiness."

I nodded, suddenly feeling sad for Zerus. I had always thought he enjoyed his own company above all else, and didn't mind that he was one of the few in The Shade of marrying age who was alone. Obviously, it mattered more than I thought.

"I'll remember that," I vowed. "But don't forget I have Aida and Serena too, and my other friends and family."

"Of course you do," he replied. "But you know I am referring to romantic love, little fae." He got up on his feet, leaning against a tree as he stood. "I am off for a night-time ramble. Leave this soon, you can always return tomorrow."

I nodded and wished him a good night. I had no intentions whatsoever of leaving the candle before I was done, but he didn't have to know that.

Once again I closed my eyes, my fingertips hovering over the jar.

"Vita!"

My name echoed across the silence of the Sanctuary, and I looked up with a start. It was Aida, waving at me. Next to her stood her brother, Jovi.

The flame in the jar leapt up, almost scorching my fingers.

"Want to walk with us?" Aida called out.

I glanced down at the flame. It had reduced back to normal, but the brown marks at the top of the jar reassured me that it hadn't just been my imagination.

"Come on!" she cried again.

I jumped up to my feet, Zerus's warning about not closing myself off from others ringing in my ears as I ran toward my friend and her wolfy brother.

SERENA
[HAZEL AND TEJUS'S DAUGHTER]

The day after my parents' acceptance of my college dreams, Aida, Vita and I were at Corrine's house having the last adjustments made to our dresses. Tonight, we, along with the rest of The Shade's residents, would be going to the In-Between to celebrate the birth of Queen Nuriya's and Sherus' baby boy. I'd been looking forward to this for weeks. I'd been to the In-Between, to the fire star, once before, but it was a long time ago, and the home of the fae held a fascination for all three of us.

"How big do you think it actually is?" I asked Corrine as

she tucked in the hem of my dress. We had been talking about the In-Between all morning, and still none of us had tired of the subject.

"I'm not exactly sure. But vast—we have very little idea of all the planets and stars that it contains, or what creatures might live there. We have only ever encountered a few, and I imagine have only scratched the surface of the species that call it home."

"The Oracle's in the In-Between, right?" I asked.

"Somewhere, yes, we believe so. As you know, we haven't heard from her since the events of Nevertide. I do sometimes wonder what happened to her…I half expected her to return to visit, but she never did."

"Our mysterious fairy godmother," Vita sighed. "I wish we could meet her. I want to know what she gifted us with."

"I don't know about gifts… I think she was just blessing you," Corrine said.

"Not sure how blessed I feel," muttered Aida, grumbling as she took in her appearance. "Why couldn't she bless me with magnetic sex-appeal, or super fighting skills? Or lack of hair, for that matter."

"Enough," Corrine scolded. She disliked it when Aida spoke badly of herself. We all did. "You, madam, have a body to die for, thick beautiful hair, and your eyes are golden, for goodness' sake—what more do you want?"

I laughed out loud. It was so true. Aida just had no clue how pretty she was. The color in her cheeks flared up at the compliment, and she fell silent. I didn't really believe the myth about the Oracle's blessing either—it had only come about because all three of our mothers had gotten pregnant at the same time, and Phoenix, Vita and Aida were born on exactly the same day... pretty much down to the same hour. It was amazing for sure, and possibly the Oracle's touch had something to do with it, but that didn't mean that they were gifted. None of them had noticed any "gifts" thus far in their lives, anyway.

"Speaking of the blessed, where is Phoenix?" Aida asked. "I haven't seen him all day, but I take it he's coming?"

I rolled my eyes. "Back in Hawaii. He's dating another girl—she works in a surf shop, of course," I replied.

"How many is that this summer?" Vita asked with a bemused expression.

"I've lost count. We're almost in the double digits though. He's so greedy."

Vita and Corrine laughed, but Aida shook her head.

"I'm not sure about that, I think Phoenix's a romantic at

heart—he secretly wants to find someone that will make him as happy as your dad and mom are," she replied with a smile. "You're all too hard on him."

"Believe that if you want," I scoffed. "But I know my brother. He'll never settle down with one woman—he loves them all too much. He's like a kid in a candy store."

Aida snorted at that, but I meant what I said. I knew he would never set out to deliberately hurt anyone, but I didn't think he'd be able to help himself.

"Okay, I'm just about finished—have a look, tell me what you think." With a wave of her hand, Corrine produced a mirror where a picture frame had been only moments before, and we all stood in silence as we surveyed her mastery.

"You really are amazing, Corrine. Thank you." I sighed softly. The dresses were beautiful. We were so lucky to have a witch in The Shade who was more than happy to make such artistic creations. The girls might refer to the Oracle as their fairy godmother, but I felt like the real one was Corrine. She had helped in each of our births, watched us grow, and had always been there—facilitating our education, soothing scratches and treating injuries with her usual calm bedside manner, and then, like today, making us appear like royalty with her unparalleled seamstress skills.

"Haven't you ever thought about becoming a world-famous fashion designer in a Paris atelier?" I asked, only half-joking.

Corrine smirked. "If I did that, who would help you?"

"It wasn't encouragement," I replied hastily, "never leave us!"

"You are a genius though, Corrine," Vita replied softly, her fingers running down the sides of her dress. Vita had the smallest frame out of the three of us, and so her dress was the simplest. It was a sheath of icy-pale blue that made her turquoise eyes pop and fell to her high-heeled feet, skimming her body. The straps were thin, showing off the delicate and pale skin of her décolletage. Her arms were left bare, her dark blonde hair tied in a low bun at the bottom of her neck. She wore a thin, silver chain around her neck that held a small fire stone amulet—a gift from her mom and dad.

Aida's dress was a different style entirely, a body hugging creation that clung to her curves and showed off her figure. The material was a darker, richer hue of blue that perfectly set off her golden eyes. Her hair was left loose, tumbling down in thick, brown waves. The dress managed to look modest and unbelievably sexy all at once—gone was the battle-strong Aida I knew, and in her place was a complete temptress.

"Wow, Aida!" I exclaimed, taking in her appearance.

"I know." She grinned. "I second Vita, you're a genius, Corrine."

I took my turn in the mirror, and was just as pleased with the results as my friends were. My dress was shorter than theirs, showing off my main asset—long legs, which kind of made up for my lack of bust and curves. It was a strapless, rich crimson chiffon-type creation that had a tight bodice, with multiple layers of skirt exploding beneath, almost like a ballet dancer's tutu. It was *incredible.* My hair was worn loose too, trailing straight down my back—it had been so long since my last haircut, it almost reached my butt.

"Do you think I should do something with this?" I picked up a clump of my hair.

Vita, Aida and Corrine all shook their heads.

"No," Corrine insisted, "you look perfect."

We all hugged Corrine, and then it was time for us to change back into our boring day-wear, go home and pack. We'd be staying overnight in Sherus' palace—another aspect of the event I was looking forward to, especially as the three of us would all be sharing a room.

"Remember to keep the dresses on a hanger before you leave," Corrine commanded us. We all nodded dutifully, all of us clinging to the fabrics like we never wanted to be parted from them.

We left Corrine's home and got ready to go our separate ways.

"See you in two hours?" I asked the girls.

"Don't be late!" Aida said.

Huh. Fat chance of *that*.

Field

My bags were already packed for tonight's trip to the In-Between, my suit hanging in my parents' house. I strode swiftly to Maura's treehouse. Maura had meant to meet me earlier this afternoon so we could wrap the gift we'd chosen for Sherus and Nuriya's child, but she'd never showed. I assumed that she'd just forgotten, but still, even that was unusual for her.

I arrived at their front door, and knocked. I could hear Orlando and Regan inside, though I wasn't sure why the former was here. Normally it would be only Regan to come round and get ready with Maura for a special occasion, since her daughters liked to be left to themselves.

Orlando opened the door and cleared his throat while standing back from the threshold.

"Hey, Field." A slight color rose in his cheeks, and he ran a finger across the inside of his shirt collar. By the state of his dress I could see that he was in the middle of getting ready. His dark eyes didn't quite meet mine.

"Sorry to bother you. Maura in?" I asked, not really understanding why he was behaving so awkwardly. I knew Orlando too well for him to be treating me like a stranger.

"Yeah, she's in her room… Do you want a drink?" he asked.

I shook my head. "Just want to see Maura. We need to be leaving soon anyway, right?" I asked.

He nodded, and then led me into the kitchen, the front door still wide open. I stared after him in puzzled bemusement, and shut the door myself. I made my way to Maura's room, at the back of the house, and quietly rapped my knuckles on the door.

"Maura?" I asked.

The door was flung open. Within an instant, Maura had flung herself in my arms, squeezing me tight, her face buried against my chest.

"You smell so good," she said, her voice muffled. I hugged her back, my hands trailing through her dark brown hair, a smile on my face. I didn't know what had gotten into the siblings, but they sure were behaving oddly. I held Maura gently, waiting for her to release me.

"Are you okay?" I asked, after she didn't move.

She nodded her head, burrowing into the crook of my neck. I glanced around her room, noticing that she hadn't packed. The bag she usually traveled with was still on top of the wardrobe, untouched.

"Aren't you feeling well?" I pressed. This time I pushed her gently away from me so that I could see her expression. She looked flustered.

"I'm fine," she breathed. Her eyes closed for a moment, and then she took a deep breath, standing back from me, leaving me standing by the door. She looked everywhere but at me, and a kick of sickness jolted through my stomach. I'd seen this expression on her face before—the last time we broke up after an argument—but never quite as flustered as now. Something was very off.

"Look at me, Maura," I said, wanting to read her gaze—wanting to know what was coming, and how much it was going to hurt.

Her eyes met mine.

I folded my arms across my chest, my throat dry.

"Field, I'm not coming tonight," she stated.

I nodded slowly.

"I can't believe I'm doing this," she continued, her voice high and tight. "You're the most incredible boyfriend. Really, you are, and I'll always, *always* love you."

I felt like someone had just punched me in the stomach.

"But," she continued, now looking at the floor, "I can't be with you anymore. It's been creeping up on me the last year, and I've realized I'm more than ready for kids. But in spite of how long it's been, I don't feel *our relationship* is ready for them...We've been stable the last two years, but I don't know what next year will look like. Now, I'm sure you'd say you'd have them with me, settle down and marry me, if I asked you to—but I also know it would only be to make me happy." Her voice broke, becoming raspy and hollow. I wanted to take her in my arms, hating to see the obvious pain whipping across her face, but I couldn't move. The sick jolt I had felt when I'd first understood what was coming had spread through my body, seizing up my muscles, so I could only stand and stare, waiting for her to deliver the final blows.

"We're not forever, Field. I think we both know that by now. We don't have the kind of steady, abiding love your parents have, or other couples I see in The Shade. I know you care for me deeply, but you don't look at me the way Ben looks at River. I know you love me, and you'd do anything to make me happy—but I want more. And I… I want *you* to have more. We both deserve that. I'm doing this because I know you never will. You would never do anything to hurt me—so I'm going to have to hurt you instead."

As the words left her, she bent double, her arms wrapped around her body as she sank onto the bed. "Please believe me when I say this is the hardest thing I've ever had to do. But I know it's the right thing."

I stood frozen, still not moving from my position by the door.

How can this be the right thing?

I could see her pain, and I could feel my own. If a permanent breakup was going to be this heartbreaking, then I just didn't understand why she felt it was the right thing to do.

"I want all the things you want—children, to settle down. I just thought we were taking our time, because we had time… lots of time, to do all that we wanted to do."

Maura shook her head.

"It doesn't work like that," she whispered. "When you're with the person…the one you're meant to be with, all the lifetimes in the world just don't seem enough."

We were silent for a long moment, Maura with her head in her hands, not wanting to look at me, me leaning on the doorframe, feeling completely powerless and reeling from her words.

I thought about the conversation I'd had with my mother, years ago. I remembered feeling reassured by the idea that Maura and I were just 'slow burners'. Our love for one another would grow over time, not the arrow that pierced straight through the heart, but the potion that slowly suffused the body—gentler, but no less valid. Not a lesser love. But clearly it hadn't been enough. That was what hurt the most. That I must have been hurting Maura all along. How long had she known that what we had wasn't real?

"You should have said something earlier," I managed. "I could have done something…made you feel more loved."

She turned to me, her face tear-stained, but with a gentle smile on her face.

"It doesn't work like that," she replied softly. "If it did, I wouldn't be doing this."

I nodded, swallowing. I didn't think I could say anymore. Her eyes reflected my own sorrow and pain, but there was also a look of resolve and determination. And perhaps more harrowing was the look of relief.

"Thank you for being honest," I said, with difficulty. I desperately needed to get out of that room, get out of the house—perhaps out of The Shade as a whole, just for a while. We both needed space and time to grieve.

"I'll always love you, Field," she said, noticing my shift in energy, indicating that I was about to leave.

"I'll always love you too," I replied quietly.

In the next moment, I had gone.

I walked in the direction of my parents' house, dragging in lungfuls of air. My entire body felt taut and heavy. I was hardly aware that one foot was stepping in front of the other. The last thing I felt like doing was celebrating the birth of a child at the fire star, but right now it seemed like the best option—my absence would be missed by my parents and my brothers. It would be easier to attend, and not have to explain anything. I wouldn't even know where to start.

Vita
[Grace and Lawrence's daughter]

When I arrived at the port, Serena and Aida were already there, looking beautiful in their gowns and chatting animatedly while they admired the splendor of the other members of GASP. I took a deep breath before I joined the crowds. Social events like this weren't exactly comfortable for me. I always felt gauche, and was paranoid that I was boring people when I joined in with small talk. I felt a wave of gratitude for my friends—what would I do without them? When I was around Serena and Aida, I could just hide behind their exuberance. Aida might have been self-conscious in front of the opposite sex, but she was naturally outgoing and loud, and Serena constantly brimmed with confidence and, no matter what the occasion, always seemed to enjoy herself.

They caught sight of me and waved me over. I turned to my mom, giving her hand a squeeze.

"See you there?" I asked.

"Of course," she smiled at me. "Just remember to have fun tonight… no running off to practice your fire abilities."

I shook my head, blushing. My mom knew me too well.

"Ah," my dad replied, raising an eyebrow in my direction, "is that why my usually reclusive daughter is so willing to join a huge social event?"

"It was," corrected my mom. "Not anymore. I want to see you on the dance floor at least once."

"All right," I held up my hands in surrender. "I'll remind you later how weird it is that you want me to party and not study…but whatever."

My mom rolled her eyes at me. "You know we think both are important. I just don't want you to miss out."

I smiled at her, giving her a quick embrace. She knew I was only teasing her, but I knew how important it was to them both that I socialized more. A lot of people had been telling me the same thing lately, I thought – remembering Zerus.

"I know, mom."

"Go, be with your friends," she replied.

I hurried to join them, narrowly avoiding Aiden and Kailyn's adoptive son Hunter commenting on how beautiful I looked. That was another thing—compliments just made me *glow* red. I smiled and waved at the werewolf as I rushed past, so as to not cause offense.

"Sorry I'm late," I huffed, plonking my bag down next to theirs.

"Don't worry," replied Serena, "it's given us a chance to people-watch. Everyone looks amazing—who knew my mom and dad could scrub up so well?"

Aida and I looked at her suspiciously.

"Err… Everyone, Serena. Your parents are insanely good looking," Aida replied, shaking her head.

Ibrahim, Corrine and Mona (with her husband Kiev next to her) were standing closest to the edge of the port, the witches and warlock waiting for everyone to arrive before transporting us. The dragons would be traveling by themselves—some were coming from The Hearthlands, with those who lived at The Shade presumably having gone on ahead already. My great grandparents Sofia and Derek were standing with my parents, along with River and Ben. They all looked so sophisticated, and inhumanly beautiful.

"Oh, look!" Serena exclaimed, as Shayla appeared with Ash and Ruby and their two kids—the boy, Varga, who was seventeen, and Elonora, a fifteen-year-old who was the spitting image of her mom. Serena rushed through the crowd to meet them, and we followed. Before we reached them, Claudia and Yuri were there, embracing their daughter and son-in-law. Both Ash and Ruby were the same sentry-and-vampire mix that Serena's parents were, but remained living in Nevertide, though they visited The Shade often.

"Serena, you've grown so much!" Ruby exclaimed, hugging her. "And where's Phoenix? Where are your parents? Where are Benedict and Yelena? And Julian?"

Hazel and Tejus appeared from behind us, and I stood back to let the old friends talk. Benedict, Yelena and their daughter Fiona had to miss this evening's event, due to an issue in the UK (Yelena's birthplace), concerning some dodgy 'Jack the Ripper' style killings that were unnerving – but we weren't entirely sure were supernatural-related, hence Benedict and Yelena going to investigate. While they were that side of the world, they'd taken Fiona to stay with Yelena's parents. As for Julian, he should be here with his girlfriend Ariana… But where was Phoenix? I glanced over at Aida, who was searching the crowd for him, but neither of us could make out his tall figure. As I scanned the crowds, my eyes lighted on Jovi, who looked very handsome in a dark suit, his dark hair brushed back off his forehead, for once, and his facial hair trimmed down to a designer stubble.

Serena was standing nearby, and I noted how beautiful she looked with her head thrown back in laughter at something Ash had said, one arm slung over the shoulder of her mother. I couldn't help but notice how many guys our age were watching her, but squashed the small flicker of jealousy I felt instantly. I loved Serena—I could hardly blame her for the fact that boys rarely noticed me. It was just because I was too shy, never appearing as carefree as Serena, or as approachable. I suddenly wished that Zerus was coming, but I already knew he had declined the invite. I could just see how the evening would go—fae princes and soldiers gathering around my friends like flies, while I awkwardly hovered by the edges of a dance floor, beyond irritated at myself for being such an introvert.

"Are you excited to be going to your birth star?" Aida turned to me, her eyes glowing.

"Yes." I grinned, reminding myself why I had been excited about this trip in the first place—the fire star was linked to my primary element, and if there was anywhere in the worlds where my abilities might be at their strongest, it was there.

"I can't wait to sleep in the palace," Aida replied, "and eat fae food. The night's going to be amazing, trust me." She gave my hand a squeeze, guessing how I felt.

Ibrahim waved to get our attention.

"Everyone gather round—we're going to depart in one minute."

Everyone muttered their assent and did as Ibrahim instructed. Serena moved to stand next between Aida and me, grasping each of our hands.

"Wait!" Serena said to her parents. "Where is Phoenix?"

Before Tejus or Hazel could reply, Phoenix's voice came from behind us. "Here." We all turned and looked up at his grinning face.

"Where have you been?" Serena scolded him.

He shrugged, still outside the circle everyone was forming. "Just finishing something up—never you mind, little sis."

Serena turned back to face her parents, who stood opposite us. "Whatever."

"Get in the circle, Phoenix," Aida muttered, and finally he did.

Corrine clapped her hands. "All right, all right. Ready everyone?"

"Ready," everyone chorused.

A moment later, we were standing on the snowy peaks of Mount Logan. I shivered, hit by the sudden extreme drop in temperature, but it would only be temporary. We all piled into the portal walled by grayish blue mist, and started to glide along—our pace kept slow by the witches' magic, to prevent the vortex from sucking us right down. Corrine gestured that we should start moving closer toward the wall of the portal, and soon we were enveloped in its thick mists, totally blinded and disorientated for a few moments until we broke through to the other side. The mists disappeared to reveal an expanse of blackness, small pinpricks of stars surrounding us as we floated through the dense silence. This part of the journey was a strange one; the stars and the great, black void were so awe-inspiring that it made me want to stay forever, but the crushing and absolute absence of noise also started to feel like it would drive me mad.

The fae planets came into view, the small spheres glowing brightly as we moved toward them. Their light bounced off the smooth skin of my friends, giving them an iridescent, unearthly appearance.

Our journey sped up, and soon we were descending onto the star. I closed my eyes briefly as the jolt of the last part of the journey made me feel slightly queasy, and when I opened them, I was standing on the ground—the magnificence of the fire star sprawled out before me.

AIDA
[Victoria and Bastien's daughter]

After my feet touched solid ground, it took me a few more seconds to comprehend the sight that greeted me. There was so much to see, so many spectacular colors and sights and smells that it was almost a violent assault to my senses.

I stared, open-mouthed, as elegant dancers swirled across the lawn, swathes of delicate scarves being waved in tempo to a jumble of musical sounds, the beat languid and soft before picking up into a bursting roll of drums and pipes. There were at least five different bands all playing at once, ensembles made up of several fae, but somehow all keeping in tune with one another. Fae guards stood to attention in rich, red robes, their weapons gleaming in the amber light that emanated from stone sculptures at various points across the grounds of the palace. Everywhere I looked, ice fires shot up into the air, their blazes almost reaching the top of the palace. Each time one of them burst alight, the heavy bushes and bouquets of flowers that were draped on the backs of chairs and table-tops suddenly seemed to come alive, as if the petals themselves were dancing along to the music.

Rows and rows of long banquet tables were laid out, their surfaces heavy with more stone sculptures and elaborate decorations of berries and flowers, along with large pieces of silverware. Off in the distance, I could see clusters of hedges, some neat and orderly, some wild and overgrown. From within them, I could hear the raucous laughter of guests. After staring, puzzled, for a few moments, I realized they were small mazes—strange lights came from inside them, and fireworks were being set off at their central points.

"How is this even more amazing than I expected it to be?" Serena murmured. I turned to her in surprise, almost forgetting that my friends were standing right next to me.

I looked toward the palace and saw Sherus and Nuriya standing on the front steps—they were accepting gifts, all piled high on a table, and greeting guests who appeared to be other fae, perhaps from the neighboring elemental stars.

"Let's go and say hello," I said, realizing that the rest of the Shadian guests were already moving to greet the couple. My parents would have brought our gifts along, but I couldn't see them in the crowd. The lights kept darting about, showing quick snapshots of one group of guests before lighting up somewhere else.

"Let's go," Serena agreed.

Before we could move, a fae appeared before us, dressed in the official livery of the fire star. He took our bags, telling Serena the directions to our room in the palace. I zoned out, too entranced with the scene around us. Serena was always better organized than Vita or I were, anyway.

When the conversation was finished, we made our way through the crowd, sticking close by one another so we didn't get lost. We kept passing faces we knew, but in the next moment they would be gone, replaced by ones we didn't—elaborately adorned fae, some dancing in abandon, some stern-faced and almost disapproving of our presence.

We waited on the steps to take our turn. Here at least the

light remained constant. Small lanterns floated in mid-air, casting a warm glow over the new family. Nuriya held the child in her arms, wrapped in silk swaddling, her face beaming as she spoke with her guests, and then her smile broadening even more as she looked down at her child. Sherus stood with one arm wrapped around her. His expression was one of pride and happiness, and every other second he turned to gaze at his wife and their new infant, as if he couldn't quite believe his luck.

"What do you think it's going to be like?" Vita whispered. "A mix of fae and jinni…its abilities are going to be *incredible*."

I nodded. There was no denying that. And a child of two royal bloodlines as well.

The couple in front of us, who I didn't recognize, moved out of the way and we took the final step up the stairs to greet our hosts.

"Girls!" Nuriya exclaimed happily. "Thank you so much for coming. You all look absolutely stunning."

"Thank you for inviting us," we gushed, all peering into the bundle that lay in Nuriya's arms.

"Do you have a name yet?" I breathed, staring down at the cherub-faced little creature who stared back up at me, his mouth forming a perfect little 'o' as he waved his chubby fist in my direction.

"We'll announce it later." Nuriya smiled. "There's a ritual that will name him for us—we let the fire element decide."

I nodded, not really understanding what she meant, but utterly transfixed by the small child. I reached out my little finger, trying to stroke his impossibly small hands. My skin touched his, and the next moment—he was gone!

"What?!" I gasped, looking up at Nuriya in panic.

The jinni queen laughed softly. "He does that sometimes. Don't worry, he'll be back in a moment."

The other two exhaled in relief, but I only felt reassured once I saw him again. Like his mother claimed, he appeared a few moments later, gurgling softly and reaching for my finger again.

I smiled weakly back at the couple, who were looking at us all in amusement. We made our excuses and left, rejoining the buzz and crowds of the party.

"That was weird," I murmured as we reached the banquet tables. "Scared me half to death."

"I think they're going to have an interesting time when he's a toddler…" Vita replied.

"Can you imagine?" Serena exclaimed. "They'll lose him every other second."

Vita said something else, but her voice was lost in the music and a particularly loud group of dancing fae that crossed our path. They were all holding on to one another, like some exotic conga procession. I smiled, waiting for them to pass.

We were about to move on when one of the fae broke away from the back of the line. He stood in front of me, blocking my path. He wore a light blue robe with a large cowl hood that shaded most of his features, all except a full-lipped mouth that was raised ever so slightly into a smile.

"Good evening," he announced, addressing me with a silken voice.

I was taken aback by the sudden approach, and it was a few moments before I could get my brain to function properly enough to muster up a reply.

"Hi," I said, trying to smile.

"See you later, Aida!" Serena dragged Vita off into the crowds, and before I could smile apologetically at the man in front of me and follow them, he had taken my hand in his and brought it to his lips. He kissed it and held it for a few moments longer than necessary before finally releasing me.

"I'm Thantos," he introduced himself, removing the heavy cowl that obscured his features. It was immediately obvious to me that he was fae. The delicate bone structure and luminescent skin couldn't belong to any other species. His eyes were a bright, piercing blue, his hair an almost white blond, drawn back from his forehead and trailing down to his shoulders.

"Nice to meet you," I replied, only just avoiding a stammer. "I'm Aida, I'm from The Shade."

"And a werewolf," he mused, his blue eyes sparkling with humor.

"What of it?" I asked. I knew that not all fae were as welcoming toward other supernaturals as Sherus and his kin were. His expression became instantly repentant.

"Nothing," he replied. "I can just sense it. It's curious to me, that's all—I wanted to meet you. I didn't know werewolves could be quite so captivating."

"I'm part werewolf," I corrected, heat rising up in my cheeks despite my best efforts to remain unruffled.

He nodded, the slow smile returning and lighting up his handsome face.

"Will you dance with me then, Aida of The Shade?"

I glanced around for my friends. They were gone.

Why not? I asked myself. I'd come here to have fun, and spending some time with an exotic fae was definitely the way to have it.

"All right," I replied. He took me in his arms, one hand sliding around my waist and the other taking my hand. As if by design, the music slowed, and a soft, mournful tune echoed across the grounds of the palace. Thankfully, he led me like an expert. I wasn't exactly skilled in ballroom dancing. Caleb had once tried to teach Serena, Vita and me, but we had made poor students, more interested in being twirled than actually learning any of the steps.

"You move beautifully," Thantos whispered in my ear, his warm breath tickling my neck. I felt like we were dancing inches off the ground… then it occurred to me that with a fae, that was actually *possible*, and I looked down to double-check. No, we were definitely on the ground. I started to relax into his arms, enjoying the haunting notes of the music, almost growing drowsy from the spicy scents of the food and the balmy air of the summer night.

"Do you have a male companion, back at home?" the fae asked.

"Um…no," I murmured, wondering why that answer

suddenly made me feel sad when it never had before. I looked out into the crowds, thinking of Field. I hadn't seen him before we left The Shade, and I couldn't see him now. But perhaps I'd just missed him and he was off in one of the mazes with Maura. They could have been dancing mere feet away from us and I still wouldn't necessarily have noticed him, thanks to the sporadic lighting.

"I can't imagine how that can be," Thantos murmured, his blue eyes searching mine.

Inwardly I scoffed. This guy was certainly a smooth talker, but there was only so much charm I could take. Still, I wasn't ready for the dance to end just yet. The weight of his hand on my waist was comforting, and just being able to enjoy a few moments with a ludicrously handsome man—one who was actually being attentive—was a feeling I wasn't willing to part with just yet.

We started to move faster and faster. The tempo of the music had picked up, and we spun around and around until I started to grow giddy. His long white hair flew around us, and I started to imagine it was the white sea foam that broke along the shore in The Shade on blustery days. I saw myself as a four-year-old girl, wearing the pink-spotted swimsuit I recognized from old pictures, carrying a plastic bucket in one hand, loading it up with shells and stones to bring back as 'treasures' to my mom.

I stumbled backward.

"Whoa," I mumbled, the image vanishing and being replaced with the spinning lights of the celebration. The ground shifted and swayed beneath my feet. I held onto the arms of the fae, trying to regain my balance.

"Are you okay? I'm so sorry. I forget that we fae move too fast for others' liking," he replied, drawing me over to a chair. He handed me a glass of water, and I drank from it greedily.

"Don't worry," I replied when I'd finished. "It's probably more to do with the journey here. The silence of the In-Between always gets to me."

He nodded solemnly.

"And when did you last eat, little wolf?"

Oh.

It had been a while ago, stupid me. I was probably hungry and dehydrated. With all the excitement of the dress fitting and then getting here, I'd forgotten to eat anything since breakfast.

"Let me get you something. Wait here," he replied, seeing my vacant expression. He left the table abruptly, and I couldn't help but feel a little bit smug that I'd found such an attentive dance partner for the evening.

FiELd

A distorted sense of reality had kicked in. I couldn't quite grasp that the last few hours had actually happened, and my mind reeled from the speed at which I'd gone from a relationship break-up to the wild and elaborate celebrations taking place on the fire star.

From the moment I landed I realized that coming here was a mistake. It was crazy to think that I could join in and match the jubilation of everyone else. My mind was a million miles away, cursing myself for failing Maura—for just not loving her enough.

Phoenix had gravitated toward me as soon as we arrived,

apparently noticing my mood. I'd told him briefly it was about Maura and he understood I wanted space. Now he and my brothers stood at the side of the dance floor, staring at some of the extraordinarily attractive fae woman with their mouths half-open. All except Sky, who was doing everything in his powers to get Aisha and Horatio's daughter, Riza, to dance with him.

"Just one dance," Sky mock-pleaded. "You're breaking my heart here, Riza."

The jinni laughed, a tinkling, musical sound that was almost drowned out by the harmony of violas and flutes from the band nearest to us.

"Your heart's robust, I'm sure you can take it," she teased.

"It's fragile!" Sky retorted, pretending to be deeply affronted. "Especially when it's in the hands of a cruel, beautiful jinni girl with amethyst eyes…"

Riza, to her credit, gave a snort of derision.

"You're ridiculous," she replied, rolling her eyes, but she couldn't hide the small smile of amusement that lit up her soft features.

"If you want me to stop, you'll have to dance with me," Sky bargained.

"Oh, heck—Riza, will you just dance with the idiot?" Blue intervened, apparently bored of his brother's pleading. Riza accepted Sky's outstretched hand with a sigh.

"I'm doing this to save your brothers from more pain," she stated, leading him on to the dance floor. Sky grinned broadly, not believing her for a second.

I joined in the laughter of my brothers and Phoenix, but my heart wasn't in it. Sky had been devoted to Riza for a long time, staying away while she was growing up, and then finally starting to pursue her when he felt the time was right. He looked at her the way my father looked at River. If Sky could manage to fall head-over-heels in love, then what was wrong with *me*?

I watched as Fly and Rock caught the attention of a group of fae girls and disappeared onto the dance floor.

"Where's Maura tonight?" Blue asked, looking around as if she might appear out of nowhere.

Phoenix cleared his throat, suddenly fascinated by a bouquet of flowers that were trailing down from the nearest stone sculpture.

"She's staying behind," I replied curtly.

"What, why?" Blue questioned.

"She's busy."

"What are you talking abo—"

"Blue, want another drink?" Phoenix asked him, interjecting.

"I'm going to see my family," I muttered, departing from the group before Blue could ask me any further questions. I knew I would have to tell my brothers soon, but not here—I knew they'd be devastated for me, and I didn't want to dampen the mood.

I wandered past the dance floor, nearer the darkened mazes. I wasn't particularly intent on finding my family—I knew how long Mom had been looking forward to tonight, and I felt my state of mind was like a poisonous thing, not to be inflicted on anyone but myself. Unfortunately, I spotted my parents just as they saw me... too late to turn away.

"There you are!" my mom exclaimed, smiling as she laid eyes on me.

"Where's Maura?" Ben asked.

"She's not coming," I replied, trying to sound as casual as I could. Mom glanced over at Ben.

"Will you go and make sure Vita's okay? I think I saw her near the palace steps, but Serena and Aida weren't with her," she said.

"Of course," Ben replied. He turned to me, looking as if he wanted to say something, but instead gave me a friendly pat on the back and strode off in the direction of the palace.

"Do you want to talk about it?' my mom asked, her gaze soft and concerned.

"Not really." I smiled wryly. "There's not a lot to say."

My mom reached out and squeezed my hand.

"I think you need to talk about it, Field. I don't like seeing you like this."

"Really, it's okay. Maura and I broke up. For good. She didn't think it was ever going to work long-term, and, you know, that's fine." I cleared my throat, annoyed at myself for worrying my mom and letting my feelings show so obviously.

"And what do *you* think?" she asked.

I sighed. I wasn't sure I knew *what* I thought. Part of me couldn't imagine what it would be like not to be with Maura, and the other part of me understood what she'd been talking about. I knew we didn't share the same intensity as quite a few couples in The Shade, but I'd just thought that was our way—that we were more casual and laid-back. Maybe I was wrong to think that way. Maybe I just didn't understand what real, life-altering, all-consuming love was like.

"It's complicated," I replied eventually, realizing how lame that sounded.

My mom was silent for a few moments, chewing on her bottom lip. Like always when she was about to give advice or her opinion on something, she was choosing her words carefully.

"I guess some relationships aren't forever. But it doesn't mean they weren't special while they lasted, that they don't mean anything. You'll always carry a bit of Maura in your heart, as she will with you. You'll have learned a lot, about how to be a partner, about how to put someone's needs before your own—whether you realize it now or not. All that you can take into the next relationship, when you're ready." She smiled at me, straightening my tie. "You've grown into an amazing young man, Field. I'm proud of you, so is your father. When you're ready to start dating again, or when you find your own 'forever,' whoever it is will be lucky to have you—and when it's the right person, you'll know, and you won't ever want to let go. You'll fight for them. Trust me."

I felt a lump forming at the back of my throat. The second of the day.

I tried to shake off the waves of emotion. It had been too

long a day already.

"I think I'll have a break from women for a while," I muttered, already weary at her suggestion of dating others.

"Of course," she replied instantly. "Work out what it is that *you* want first, before jumping into anything else."

"I will," I promised. I hadn't the faintest clue what I wanted right now. Other than to be single for a really, really long time. Maybe I needed to take some tips from Phoenix in that department—he seemed able to enjoy the company of the opposite sex without getting entangled too deeply…then again, maybe not. I smiled to myself. Phoenix's style wasn't really mine.

Grace and Lawrence came into view, weaving their way through the dance floor till they reached us.

"Did you go in the maze?" Grace asked excitedly. "I was lost in there for about an hour. I tried to drag Hazel with me, but she point-blank refused."

"Shall we try one?" my mom asked, looking up at me.

"Let's do it," Lawrence said with a grin. "All of us."

I shrugged. Why not? Maybe family time was what I needed right now… as well as keeping clear of my Hawk brothers' raging testosterone and their affinity for the perfectly-formed fae.

SERENA
[HAZEL AND TEJUS'S DAUGHTER]

Oh. My. God.

I couldn't believe what I'd just overheard.

Leaping up from my seat, I searched the crowds for Aida. If Field had broken up with Maura for good, she'd want to know right away. I moved off toward the dance floor to see if she was still with the fae boy who had picked her up earlier, but I couldn't see either of them. Accidentally, I bashed into Victoria, who was moving past me.

"Whoa, Serena—where's the fire?" She laughed good-naturedly, holding me at arm's length.

"Sorry!" I blustered. "Just trying to find Aida."

"She's around here somewhere," Victoria replied. "I saw her dancing with a rather handsome-looking fae earlier." She winked at me, smiling to herself before being called for by her mother, Vivienne.

I carried on, weaving my way through the couples on the dance floor, but moving at a slower pace. The interruption was enough to make me rethink my actions. I was treating Field's heartbreak like gossip when it really wasn't. By the sounds of it, Field was devastated by the news, and my heart went out to him. And Maura. They had been together, albeit on and off, for *ages*. I couldn't imagine what it was like to share so much history with someone and then have it all end like that. A few words spoken, and then *bam*—the world as you knew it, over.

I would tell Aida—I knew her feelings for the Hawk were genuine—but I would do it tactfully, not rushing over and divulging the news breathlessly. Still. I couldn't help the adrenaline running through me as I thought that my friend might finally have a chance with the man of her dreams.

I spied Aida through the crowds. One of the ice sculptures flared up suddenly, capturing the image of Aida and the hot fae sitting at one of the banquet tables, their heads leaned toward one another as they absent-mindedly picked food off their plates.

"Serena, now's your chance." Jovi appeared next to me, his eyes lit with good humor.

"My chance for what?" I asked, slightly taken aback by his sudden appearance and how cool he looked in formal wear. His white shirt contrasted with his slightly tan skin and the dark stubble that covered his jaw. For once, his hair was neatly combed back—giving him a slightly less feral appearance than usual. I actually thought Jovi looked better when he was unkempt, but this made a nice change.

"To dance with me," he replied cockily. I smiled despite myself.

"I'm busy. Maybe later?" I asked, glancing over his shoulder in the direction of Aida and the fae. I didn't want to lose them in the crowd.

"You're busy at a dance?" he teased. "I think that's the worst excuse I've ever heard."

"But it's the truth," I objected.

I took another glance at Aida. She was laughing now. The fae was obviously a good date. He also looked completely infatuated by her. Did I want to break that up with news of Field's break up? It wasn't like she was going to shoot off immediately to console him. Field would need some time to heal before anything new came into his life— I'd heard him say so himself.

This time, Jovi followed my gaze. "Huh," he commented, "who's that?"

A frown appeared on his brow at the sight of the fae. I recognized over-protective brother impulses when I saw them.

"You're right." I said quickly, grabbing his arms to capture his attention. "Let's dance."

Vita
[Grace and Lawrence's daughter]

I'd left Serena at a seat at one of the banquet tables, telling her I'd come back to find her. The music and the lights had started to feel like too much, and the balmy night was making my head feel fuzzy. I decided to venture inside the palace, where it would be quieter, and hopefully cooler.

There were a few fae standing guard at the entrance, but they didn't try to stop me from entering. They merely bowed their heads in greeting, while one opened the tall doors for me to pass on through. The fae fascinated me, and I'd always longed to know a bit more about the way that they lived in their natural habitat. My mom and dad had both told me that I was welcome to visit the In-Between and stay with Sherus and Nuriya if I wished to, and I did, but I had always felt that it wasn't the right time. I wanted to be in full command of my abilities before I did that— not wanting the other fae to sneer at my lack of skill. It was probably an unfair assumption, but I did think it would be ten times more enjoyable if I could feel part of their kind when I visited, and not such an outsider.

The door shut behind me, and I stepped forward into the grand entrance, marveling at the ruby lights and fire stones that covered everything in a warm, yellow and red glow. The staircases were made from brilliant white marble, and the tall, pointed window frames appeared to be carved out of silver-gold metal. No wonder the entity that had plagued Nevertide had been eager to gain control of the fae lands. There was richness here beyond compare. The fae never saw it that way—to them it was just natural resource that came to them easily, and they admired it for its aesthetic qualities and the link to their elemental magic. But as someone part human, I could recognize the wealth that Sherus and Nuriya enjoyed.

Not really knowing where I was going, I started to peer

into the rooms that led off from the entrance. Most of these were unlocked, and all were empty of fae. I looked in on a few dining rooms and a study, but nothing really held my interest till I walked to the furthest end of one of the corridors and pushed open a set of double doors which were engraved with depictions of planets and stars.

I soon discovered that the room was circular—perfectly so, with a large dome rising from the top of it. The dome depicted a night's sky, covered with stars and other planets far off in the distance. I stared at it in wonder, not sure whether it was a painted image. As I drew closer to the center of the room, I realized that the image was being projected by a large, amethyst-colored stone. I crouched down, trying to work out how it was being accomplished, but all I could see was a powerful bolt of steady light shining out from its center. I turned back up to the sky, trying to understand if the image was moving—if it was a live feed or not. I couldn't be sure. Sometimes I thought I saw a star shift out of the corner of my eye, or something grow a little brighter, but it could have just been my imagination.

Making sure the door was shut and I was totally alone, I lay down on the stone floor, staring up at the cosmos. The marble of the floor was ice-cold against my back, but it was a pleasant relief after the heat of outside, and anyway, I was transfixed. I didn't think I could have moved if I'd wanted to.

Sometime after, the door creaked open. Sitting bolt upright, I turned my head, ready to apologize for my intrusion to whatever stony-faced guard appeared. I exhaled in relief as I recognized my grandfather Benjamin stepping into the room.

He smiled at me as he approached, and then turned his gaze to the ceiling.

"Impressive, isn't it?" he remarked.

"What is it?" I questioned, keeping my voice at a whisper. There was something about the room and the awe I felt in the presence of the cosmos that made me want to keep my voice at a respectfully low level.

"It's the In-Between," he replied. "As far as we can see from where we are. This stone is linked to another that hovers above the atmosphere of the fire star, sending the memories and images of one stone back to the other."

I looked up again, more spellbound now that I understood what it was I was seeing. The sky went on for lifetimes, with millions and millions of planets and stars in the distance—some nothing more than the faintest pinpricks of light.

"We really don't know much about it, do we?" I asked, recalling what Corrine had said about its sheer mass and mystery.

"Next to nothing," my grandfather agreed with a smile. "This is my favorite room in the palace. After Nevertide I often visited Sherus and Nuriya, and would always make sure I entered this room, no matter how brief my stay. It reminds me how small we are in the grander scheme of things. How can any concerns of mine weigh on my mind when I see this? It is a place for true reflection."

I nodded. I could understand what my grandfather meant, but the sight of the cosmos didn't make my own existence seem small in comparison—it made me want to explore, to know each and every star in its great mass, to unearth the creatures that might live there.

"Why have none of the fae ventured out there?" I asked. If I could fly, nothing would hold me back from journeying into the unknown.

"I think they have, partway, but the In-Between is so vast, Vita. It would take lifetimes to reach some of its planets. As a rule, the fae don't tend to go seeking out danger."

"No, I guess they don't," I murmured. I looked to one of the brightest stars that shone, far off in the distance. Surely a little risk would be worth it?

"We should head back," my grandfather replied suddenly. "They are about to commence the naming ceremony."

I rose to my feet, shaking out the cramp in my back from lying on the floor. My stomach gave a short rumble, and I realized I needed to eat—badly.

"Let's go," I replied, holding the door open for my grandfather to exit first. I shut the door behind us, glancing up one last time at the sky.

SERENA
[HAZEL AND TEJUS'S DAUGHTER]

"I'm never going to eat again," I swore, rubbing my aching stomach.

"You're not the only one," Vita replied. Aida said nothing, just nodded in agreement with a small groan as we made our way to our sleeping quarters in the palace after the ceremony. Phoenix was behind us, speaking to one of the fae girls in a low, soothing voice. It was the same way he spoke to Lucifer at home, and I wanted to laugh—did he try out his pick-up techniques on our *cat*?

"Do you know which one's ours?" Aida asked, looking

blankly at the rows of identical doors that we passed along the corridor.

"Yes," I replied smugly. "I asked the guy who took our bags to tie a ribbon around the doorknob so we'd find it again—I remember getting lost here as a kid."

Both Aida and Vita looked impressed.

After a few minutes of traipsing down the hallway, I saw the blue ribbon tied in a neat little bow on one of the doors.

"Phoenix, you're next to us." I pointed out his room, and he nodded his thanks, returning to continue charming his date. I pushed the door open, letting Aida and Vita walk in first. I followed, closing the door before I had to witness my brother saying 'goodnight' to his fae friend.

The room was huge, with three four-poster beds carved out of marble standing in the center, and two adjoining bathrooms leading off from the main sleeping area. The windows were high and pointed into elegant arches, letting in the crisp moonlight.

"Wow." Aida sighed. "This place is amazing...why are we only staying one night again?"

"Because that's the time we were invited for." I laughed, sharing my friend's wish. One night just wasn't enough time to properly enjoy the place.

"Look at the tub!" Vita exclaimed from inside one of the bathrooms. We both followed her in, sighing in amazement as we admired the grandeur of the white marble bathroom, with a tub sunken into the floor. Instead of a hand basin, there was a small collection of fire stones, and water gently trickled out of their cracks like a waterfall and collected in a small rock pool below.

"Fluffy robes!" crowed Aida, taking one off the back of the door. "This is going to be heaven."

She whipped out of one bathroom and into the other, presumably changing. Vita walked back into the bedroom, picking up Aida's high-heeled shoes from the floor and neatly lining them up next to her own. I smiled, taking the two other robes.

"We're all wearing them," I commanded. "We need to take full advantage of everything while we're here, or it's just a wasted journey."

"Good call," Vita agreed, grabbing the robe as I threw it over. As she took it, her face screwed up in pain.

"Are you okay?" I asked.

She nodded. "Yeah...fine. I think I've just eaten too much. I feel a bit odd. But I think it's the journey over here as well."

"So do I," Aida agreed, emerging white and fluffy from the bathroom. "I almost passed out on the dance floor earlier. I thought it was just lack of food…obviously not."

"Good thing you had Prince Charming to attend to you." I smirked, wiggling my eyebrows suggestively.

Aida ignored me, collapsing back on the bed with a theatrical sigh. "He was *amazing*," she breathed, staring up at the ceiling. I quickly undressed and changed into my pajamas and then put on the fluffy robe. I didn't know if now was the right time to tell her about Field and Maura. She was obviously into the fae, and from what I'd seen, the feelings weren't unrequited…like they were with Field. At least for the moment.

"What was his name?" I asked, wanting to hear more about her admirer before I made my decision.

She sat up, looking guilty and confused.

"What?" I exclaimed, laughing. "You don't know his *name?*"

"I do," she retorted. "It was 'Th' something…Thantos! That was it! *Thantos* was an excellent dancer, and a very charming man," she replied airily. I rolled my eyes, punching in the pillows on my tightly made bed to get comfortable before hearing the rest of the story.

"Did either of you see Field tonight?" Aida asked instead, her tone trying to sound nonchalant.

"I didn't actually." Vita shook her head and turned toward me. "Did you?"

"Yep," I announced, pausing. Maybe now *was* the time… "There's actually something I wanted to tell you about him."

Aida sat up, her attention solely focused on what I was about to say.

"He and Maura have split up for good," I said. "I heard him telling River about it. She broke it off earlier this afternoon, which is why she didn't attend tonight."

I waited for Aida to say something, but neither girl muttered a word.

"Poor Maura," Aida murmured eventually, her cheeks flushing a bright pink. "And poor Field. He must be heartbroken."

I nodded. "Yeah, I think he is. But he won't be forever."

Aida looked up at me, her eyes widening.

"He'll never see me that way, Serena," she replied solemnly. "I'll always just be a younger kid to him—not a girl he's seriously going to think about dating."

"What makes you say that?" I replied, the objection

obvious from my tone. I didn't believe Aida for a second.

"Because he's known me too long. I'm officially friendzoned—I think I'd be able to tell if he liked me, and I know for a fact that he doesn't," Aida replied, firm in her convictions.

"Sorry, Aida, but I don't believe that." Vita joined in. "You don't know what's going to happen. Obviously, it's not going to be right now—he's going to be hurting—but that doesn't mean it's a never."

"Exactly," I agreed, always pleased when Vita took my side, as she tended to be the voice of reason. "And if Field doesn't notice you, then he's an idiot. He won't know what he's missing," I added stoutly.

Aida's blushes increased, but before she could say anything in reply, she doubled over in pain on the bed, clutching her stomach with a grimace.

"What did you two *eat*?" I asked, immediately worried. "Shall I go and get someone—your parents?"

Aida waved her hand away. "No, don't bother them, it's probably just a stomach bug or something. The fae have rich food as well, it might be that."

"I'm going to get you both a glass of water. Just stay in bed."

Vita was starting to look even more pale than usual. I hurried into the bathroom, finding water glasses in a cabinet and filling them up from the fountain. I carried them back, hurrying as Aida let out a weak groan.

"Here," I said, handing the first to Vita and then taking the other to Aida. "Are you sure I can't do something? You both look terrible."

"Thanks," Aida muttered sarcastically.

"Don't get anyone. I think I just need to sleep it off," Vita replied, lying back on the bed. I felt her forehead. It was warm, but I couldn't tell if that was just the weather or an actual fever.

"I'm going to open the windows," I stated, and, not hearing any protest from either of them, I walked over to the glass arches and tried to find an opening latch. Once I did, I wriggled it free and the frames sprang open, bringing in a sudden gust of music and laughter from the remaining guests. The party was still in full swing below. We were high up, so I couldn't see too much till I forced my True Sight to kick in. Then I could see the dishevelment of those remaining. I smiled to myself as I watched two fae chasing one another around the dance floor, adults behaving like children. As I leaned out further, I felt a wave of hunger running through me—not for food, but the strange and powerful energy that had been radiating off the fae all evening.

No one will notice if I just take a bit...

I tried to never syphon off someone without them knowing. It was a strict rule in our house never to use the other members of The Shade like that without them knowing, and the same would apply here. Of course, in the privacy of our home it was different. We would all syphon off one another if needed, but we had to be courteous; no one would borrow my energy before I had exams, or Phoenix's before training.

But who will know?

I closed my eyes, ignoring the thoughts. It was just instinct, and it could be overcome. Thankfully, Aida groaned again, and the desire to feed was cut off abruptly.

"Do you need more water?" I asked, before noticing her still-full glass by the side of the bed.

"No," she moaned. "Shut the window though, I'm getting cold."

"Aida, it's boiling out there and in here—if you're cold you've definitely got a fever!"

I made sure she was covered in blankets, but when I went

to feel her temperature, she didn't seem overly hot. Next, I moved over to Vita's bed. Her face was starting to bead with perspiration, and the blankets had been thrown aside.

"Vita, are you okay?" I ventured, hoping I wasn't going to wake her. Her eyes were closed, but were moving rapidly beneath her lids.

"Mmm," she murmured. "I'm fine—just need to sleep it off."

This was starting to get weird. It wasn't food poisoning; I knew that much. I began to make my way toward the door. I was going to get their parents and Corrine. Clearly there was something seriously wrong with both of them, but it was something that Corrine could no doubt sort out in a second.

Field

After getting lost in the maze about a hundred times I finally located the exit with my mom—we'd lost all sight of Grace and Lawrence in the process. Dad was waiting by the exit, rolling his eyes in amusement.

"Really, it took you that long?" he asked us both archly.

"Mom wouldn't let me fly!" I laughed. "I'd like to see you do any better—without supernatural abilities, of course."

"Yeah, tough guy," my mom teased. "You can talk big, but you would have been just as lost as we were. I'm pretty sure there was jinni magic being used…I heard that the

Oracle managed to create a similar experience in Nevertide."

That made sense. No wonder Hazel had refused to join in. I could imagine that a Nevertide maze would haunt anyone for a long time.

"Did you find Vita?" Mom asked.

"I did. She was in the observatory. Curious kid, that one," he remarked, looking pleased.

"Good," Mom replied. "Now, will you please escort me to our room? I am absolutely exhausted and I am not waiting around for this party to end, because I think it's going to be dawn before it does."

"Of course," Ben replied. "What are you going to do, Field?"

"I'm going to find Sky and the rest of them, and then do the same. I'm tired."

I said goodnight to both of them, and made my way back to the place that I'd last seen them. They hadn't gone far. Phoenix was gone, but the others were there, and they'd been joined by Jovi. There weren't any fae girls to be seen, but they were all looking pretty pleased with themselves, draining glasses of some strange pink concoction that fizzed like soda when they placed it to their lips.

"Anyone ready to call it a night?" I asked.

"Already?" Rock cried. "The night's just begun. The party's just getting started!"

I sighed, rubbing my brow. I wasn't going to be the one responsible for breaking up the merriment, and it was probably best that I just left them to it. It was most likely that they'd want to sleep outdoors anyway. I had a room waiting for me—one I was meant to be sharing with Maura.

"I'll come," Jovi replied sleepily. "I've had enough. See you all in the morning."

He half-heartedly waved at the rest of the Hawks, before we both started to move in the direction of the castle.

"Good night?" Jovi asked.

I shrugged. "It was fine," I replied.

"I'm sharing a room with Phoenix," Jovi muttered. "I hope he's remembered that… and he's alone."

I laughed. It was unlikely.

"You can use mine if you need a place to crash," I offered.

We strode along the corridors, going up to the second floor where the rooms were located. Both of us were silent. The doors all looked so similar, the corridor almost impossibly long, and I half-wondered if it was some kind of fae illusion that made the interior of the palace seem even larger than it appeared from the outside.

"I don't know how I'm going to find my room," I mumbled, checking to see if I recognized any of the ornaments that hung on the walls, or the small stone sculptures that were suspended from the ceilings.

"They should have numbers on them or something," Jovi replied. He smirked. "Maybe it's designed for people to stumble in on the wrong rooms..."

I put my hand up to silence him for a moment. I'd heard some strange groaning coming from one of the rooms, as if someone was in pain.

"What is that?" Jovi replied, picking up on the noise.

We reached the door where the sound was coming from, and I could distinctly hear Serena's voice. Before I could knock and ask if everything was okay, the door swung open and Serena stood in its frame. Her body was swallowed by a large fluffy robe, which would have looked comical if her face hadn't been fraught with anxiety and distress.

"What's wrong?" I asked.

"The girls," she replied, her voice pitched high.

Before she could say another word, a loud thump came from inside the room. Jovi and I moved past her, and I saw Vita, lying on the floor next to her bed. Her body tautened for a moment, the small frame of the human-fae stretched out, her muscles tensed. We rushed toward her as she started to jerk, her body contorting in some kind of fit.

"Roll her on her side!" Jovi cried out.

We moved her, trying to be as gentle as possible, but holding her firmly so that she didn't hurt herself.

"Serena, get a pillow!" I told the girl, waiting till she dragged one from the bed and placed it beneath her friend's head. Vita's convulsing continued, her body jerking violently. I was about to tell Serena to start knocking on doors for help when Aida let out a howl.

Jovi looked over at his sister in astonishment, his face paling.

"What the hell?" he breathed, jumping up to race over to her bedside. It looked like Aida was experiencing a similar thing to Vita. Her body had arched upward off the sheets, her limbs stiff as the howl continued.

"It almost looks like she's turning," Serena exclaimed. "What is *happening*?"

"Of course she's not turning!" Jovi replied, trying to soothe his sister and roll her over into the recovery position before she started fitting in the same manner as Vita. It was horrible. I glanced briefly at Serena—she was traumatized, and I half worried that she was about to succumb to the same mysterious state as her friends.

"Serena, go and get help—just run down the corridor, knock on all the doors!" I commanded her. The girl raced to the door, but before she'd stepped through its frame, the room was blinded in a flash of bright, yellow light.

SERENA
[HAZEL AND TEJUS'S DAUGHTER]

I saw a blinding flash of light, and closed my eyes against it. A jolt in the pit of my stomach followed swiftly, making my insides feel like they were being squeezed, all the blood rushing from my head. The light vanished, and I slowly opened my eyes, turning around to see if the others had just shared the same experience.

They were gone.

Or I was.

I glanced wildly around the room, too panicked to fix my focus on one thing. It was different. I wasn't in the fae palace, or if I was, it was a different location entirely to the one I'd just been in.

Where am I?

My brain just couldn't compute that a moment ago I'd been about to leave my room, and now I was standing in a completely different one…and my friends! Vita and Aida… where were they?

I closed my eyes, taking a deep breath.

Focus, Serena.

I tried to steady my racing heart. When I was ready I opened my eyes again, and started to properly observe the room I was now in. One of the strangest things, which indicated that I was no longer in the fae palace or even on the fae star, was the fact that outside it was daylight. I walked over to the nearest window, one of three dusty glass frames that ran alongside the room. Peering out, I saw a pale blue sky. Where it met the land on the horizon, I saw miles of rich, verdant forest—more like a jungle, if anything. In some places the green was so bright it was almost neon, the trees and plants wide-leaved and tall, growing thickly in some places, and in others parting to make way for streams and the natural slope and rise of the land. It went on for miles, bands of heated haze blurring its sprawl off into the distance.

Directly below me—I must have been on the second or third floor of a brick house—there was a lawn. It was wild and overgrown, some patches burnt by the sun, the grass growing tall and unchecked in others. Around the edge of the lawn, the grass was overtaken by swampland. Trees grew from the muddy earth, their thick roots dipping down into the murky waters, vines strangling their trunks and moss hanging limply from their branches, looking like wet rags.

Where am I?

This place looked like a strange dreamland, the colors and humidity far removed from what I was used to. Turning away from the window, I studied the room I was in, hoping it might provide more clues. It was old, that much I could gather straight away. The room had been painted white, once, and now was yellowing in places with plaster coming away at the corners. The wainscoting, in a pale blue paint that matched the sky, was bubbling and peeling in the heat. The decoration in the room was simple and sparse, a large, iron-framed bed in the middle with mildew-stained white sheets. A cupboard stood in one corner, made of polished pine, next to an old-fashioned dresser. I inspected them, the creaking of the wooden drawers echoing too loudly for comfort, but both proved to be empty anyway. There was a small fireplace at one end, not swept clean—the ashes were so pale with age that they resembled little more than dust.

Finding even fewer answers in the room, I picked up an old poker by the fireside and decided to explore the rest of the house. My one small, iota of hope was that I wouldn't be alone here... I couldn't hear anyone, the silence had so far been almost deafening, but that didn't necessarily mean I was alone. With a slightly shaking hand I held the poker as firmly as I could, and pushed the door to the bedroom open.

It opened into a corridor, about eight yards or so in length. It was gloomy here, with no windows opening out into the sunshine. It was cooler though, and I stepped out of the bedroom. I waited, trying to hear something, anything, that might indicate the presence of another.

When only silence remained, I moved further along. As my eyes became accustomed to the gloom, I started to notice more evidence of a once-grand home turned shabby and worn from neglect. I also became much, much more afraid.

The hallway was wide, and on either side of me objects

and bookcases were piled high so that the house started to resemble a junkyard. I jumped as I caught sight of two beady-looking eyes staring down at me from a shelf, only to realize, in disgust, that it was an animal that had been preserved and stuffed—it looked like a fox, its body frozen mid-jump, its teeth and claws out and ready to pounce on its prey. I started to notice more examples of foul taxidermy, creatures that I recognized as belonging to Earth: snakes, lizards, owls, even a yellowed swan. I peered more closely at the books on the shelves. The volumes were thick and old, their pages yellowed. My heart sank as I made out the text. These were written in a language that I didn't recognize, and didn't perceive as belonging to Earth—unless it was some ancient text I wasn't familiar with, like Sanskrit. I slid the book back where I'd found it, and froze.

I could hear footsteps coming from the opposite end of the corridor. As I couldn't see anything, I assumed it was coming from one of the rooms. I used True Sight, searching the rooms on my left. The first two were empty of occupants, but in the last, I saw a familiar figure and almost wept with relief.

SERENA
[HAZEL AND TEJUS'S DAUGHTER]

Hurrying along the corridor, I opened the door, causing Jovi to spin around in surprise, wielding a glass vase as a weapon.

"It's me!" I hissed. "It's okay."

Jovi lowered the vase with a huge sigh of relief.

"What is this place?" he asked me. "Are you okay? I was trying to help Aida, then was practically blinded by the light—"

"Same here," I replied. "When I opened my eyes again, I was here. And I can't tell for the life of me where 'here' is."

His room was the same as mine had been, though slightly larger, with a fireplace at either end. It also had velvet curtains hanging from each of its windows, half-eaten by moths and decay.

"Wherever we are, I want to get out." Jovi made a move toward the door I'd just arrived from, and together we stepped back into the hallway.

"Do you think the others are here?" I asked hopefully. If Jovi and I had both arrived in the same place, then there was a chance the others had too.

"Did you look in other rooms?" he asked.

"They're empty," I confirmed, "there's no one else on this floor. We should try downstairs. I passed a staircase. This way." I led him on, back down the gloomy corridor.

"Look up," he whispered, coming to a standstill a few feet from the banister. I did as he asked, and quickly wished I hadn't. The ceiling was covered with murals: oil-painted depictions of black-eyed demons locked in battle with serpents and humans. Winged creatures, scaled and furious, lashed at one another, while glad-masked figures stood by and watched, as if they were at a play. It was creepy.

"Come on," I said, tugging at his shirt sleeve. I wanted to get out of here—back into the light, at least. The gloom and the watching eyes of the stuffed creatures were making me edgy.

The staircase was wide, thickly carpeted like the hallway was. Some of the steps were broken in, the polished wood of the banisters also destroyed in some places, the railings draped in thick and musty cobwebs.

"Mind your step," Jovi muttered as we slowly descended, anxious that every creak might give us away to whoever or whatever owned this place. The staircase led down to what I assumed was the main entrance. It was a vast and empty hall, whose floor was made of cracked, polished marble slates. Large paintings hung from the walls, covered in a thick layer of dust and depicting pastoral scenes—a nice change from what we'd seen on the ceiling upstairs.

Jovi hurried to the front door. It was huge, with two marble columns on either side, and rusted brass knobs on both doors. Jovi wiggled the handles, and I joined him, looking closely at the locks.

"Locked shut," I asserted, rattling the frame. In our desire to get out, I'd stopped worrying about the noise we were making. "We should just break the glass of one of the windows, it will be easier."

"Agreed," Jovi replied. "Let's see if we can find any sign

of the others first. Which way should we go?"

I turned and faced the interior of the house. The layout was vast. There were so many rooms, most cast in darkness where the curtains were pulled tightly shut. I could see one fire blazing in one of the rooms in the west 'wing' of the home, but it looked as empty as the rest. I could also see a glass greenhouse that backed onto the lawn—full of tropical hot plants, and as overgrown as the rest of the land.

I told Jovi what I saw, both of us worried that the rest of our friends and family were nowhere to be found.

"Let's make our way to the room with the fire," he suggested. "If we can't see anyone, we can get out through the greenhouse."

I led the way, glancing into the different rooms that we passed—some vast, with the furniture covered in more mildewed sheets, and some smaller, containing nothing more than chests of more junk, books and unfamiliar objects that looked like they belonged at an antique fair.

"Do you think this is some sort of trick? Maybe one of the fae playing with us or something?" I asked hesitantly.

"It'd be a pretty cruel trick," Jovi replied. "And I don't know…it would take a lot of power—a jinni would have to be involved… and all this for amusement? It doesn't sound likely."

I had to agree. And there was nothing about this that felt remotely amusing. The more we explored of the isolated home, the more disheartened I felt—and frightened. With all the panic of seeing my friends in that state, and the dancing and fun beforehand, and now the use of True Sight to keep watch on the house as we walked through it, my energy was fast depleting. If I didn't find energy to eat soon—and I didn't believe that there would be anything in this place—I would have to ask Jovi if I could syphon off him. Something I absolutely didn't want to do in this situation.

As we approached our destination, I could hear the faint sounds of a fire crackling in the hearth. I was already perspiring heavily—the house, even when cast in gloom, was humid and dank. Why anyone would want to light a fire in this heat was beyond me.

The door to the room was shut. I glanced over at Jovi, and he motioned for me to stand back. With my energy draining and the room in darkness, I couldn't see that well, but I could make out a high-backed chair, placed in front of the fire.

"Jovi," I whispered quietly before he opened the door,

"there might be someone in there. I think I can see—"

Jovi didn't wait for me to finish. On hearing that there might be a sign of life, Jovi pushed the door open with a bang. He marched into the room, and I followed him—my gait was much less confident, but that didn't mean I wasn't ready for battle.

Jovi came to a halt halfway between the door and the chair. There was definitely someone sitting in it, but they made no motion to rise at our approach. The only light came from the fire, and as a log fell on the hearth, I could make out a human hand on the armrest, unmoving.

Then a voice echoed across the room:

"So, you've found me."

SERENA
[Hazel and Tejus's daughter]

Neither of us moved.

Jovi glanced over at me, his wide-eyed gaze meeting mine.

"Who are you?" Jovi asked, in a voice stronger and more forceful than anything I could muster. The occupant of the chair didn't move. By the sound of his voice, he was definitely male—but beyond that, even using my failing True Sight, I couldn't get much of a picture.

He didn't reply to Jovi's question. The werewolf lost his temper, anger clearly overcoming whatever fear he might have entertained, and continued to march over to the chair. I followed him, our hands becoming tightly clasped as we reached the fire in a few short strides, turning toward the faceless voice.

My body was tensed for attack, but as I laid eyes on the figure, the fight drained out of me. My first reaction was one of an uneasy awe. The figure in the chair was a man— and an undeniably handsome one. His face was harsh, but young; he couldn't have been much older than his early twenties. His eyes, narrowed in a frown, were a steely gray, boring into us with mistrust. Overgrown stubble covered his jaw. His dark blond hair was worn long, stopping at the nape of his neck, shorter strands framing his jaw and temples in disarray. His frame was broad, muscular, and for some reason—perhaps it was the scent of musky heat that emanated off him like sweet hay, or the golden tan on his forearms—I got the impression that he was used to outdoor labor. If he was the owner of this grand house, that struck me as strange.

The only aspect of him that was less than harsh, and almost appeared out of place with the rest of his appearance, was his full lips, set in a perfect cupid's bow. My eyes shifted away from staring at them for any longer than a split second, disturbed at my own reaction to them.

When I realized that I was no longer afraid of the man, my immediate reaction was one of rage, one that was clearly shared with Jovi.

"Who *are* you?" Jovi demanded. "What have you done with us, and our friends?"

The man shifted his gaze to Jovi. I hadn't fully realized that while I had been staring at him, he had been assessing me with the same degree of intensity. It was only as his attention shifted that I felt able to speak, my anger tumbling out.

"Speak to us!" I said, when the man remained silent. "Where are we?"

The man sighed, his attention flitting to our clasped hands. It felt like his gaze burnt them, instantly making me want to release Jovi, so I held on tighter, not willing to be animated like a puppet by this stranger.

"Before you vent your rage at me, understand that I have performed a great service on behalf of your friends—they were in great danger at the fae palace," the man replied after a pause, his voice low and gravelly.

At the mention of my friends, I instantly changed tack.

"Where are they? Are they here?" I asked. I hadn't seen

them as I'd looked through the house.

"They are here," he replied. "Safe."

"Where? Take us to them!" Jovi demanded, losing patience with the outwardly calm attitude of the man.

"You won't like what you see," the man replied with a sigh, as if our panic was tedious to him, and something that he didn't have the patience to deal with.

"What does that mean?" I snapped, irritated at his vague answers and general attitude.

"It means I will show them to you, but you need to try to remain calm—and listen to me first," he announced, rising to his full height from the chair. He was about a head taller than me, and I'd been correct about his frame being broad; as he rose, he seemed to engulf both Jovi and me with his presence.

"We're listening," Jovi replied, his voice taking on a growl of warning.

The man nodded, turning away from us both and proceeding to walk toward a door, different to the one we'd entered through, at the far end of the room.

"Your friends are going through a state of transformation," he continued. "It was already beginning before I could reach you. I took them to save them from a fate that would be a great deal worse than death—left on the fae star, they would have very shortly been taken by creatures far deadlier than me."

"What kind of transformation?" I asked, while at the same time perplexed that a creature I so far understood to be human would know about the fae star…and manage to spirit away supernaturals from it.

"You will see."

He opened the door, revealing a set of narrow stone steps leading down into more darkness. I glanced at Jovi. He nodded, indicating that we should follow the man. It was worth taking the risk to find our friends.

The man lit a lamp on the wall with a match. The light didn't do much to lift the gloom of the stairwell, but it was better than nothing. As we followed the man down, I started to syphon off him as gently as I could. I didn't want him to realize what I was doing till it was too late. As I mentally reached out for his energy, I started to realize he wasn't as human as I'd first thought. He was a supernatural of some kind, but nothing that I recognized. Still, his energy was heady and powerful—almost as warming and enriching as sunlight itself.

"Stop that," he intoned, pausing on one of the steps.

Jovi and I quickly looked at one another.

"Stop what?" I asked.

"Whatever it is you're doing. What are you, anyway?" He spun around, glaring at me. "I know you're a werewolf," he added dismissively, waving his hand at Jovi, "but *you* are something else entirely."

"I don't know what you mean," I replied, determined not to divulge any information that he might be able to use against us.

He smirked at me, a cruel, calculating glance, but said nothing further, continuing his descent to the bottom of the staircase. I stopped syphoning, realizing I was pushing my luck. I tried to use True Sight to better understand where he was taking us, but there was only one room ahead—with a wooden door, looking as old and crumbling as the rest of the house. The only disturbing thing about it was I couldn't see through it. The door or the walls around us. I stopped, unwilling to follow the man any further.

"Jovi, wait." I grasped the material of his shirt. "I think this is a trick."

Both Jovi and the stranger spun around to face me.

"There's no trick," the man replied before Jovi could ask me what was wrong. He looked speculatively at me for a moment. I could see he was wondering what abilities I possessed, and then his eyes lit up in understanding.

"The room we're about to enter is heavily guarded. Not by living souls, but by ancient wards that you couldn't possibly comprehend. If you have a gift of advanced sight"—his lip twitched as he registered my look of frustration—"it will be useless here. My sincerest apologies," he added smoothly, returning his attention to the door. He took out a set of keys. Jovi and I watched, standing side by side, ready for anything that might emerge from the locked room.

A key clicked in the lock, and presently the door swung open. The man stood aside, gesturing for us to enter.

"You first," Jovi snapped. The man nodded, crossing the threshold. We both followed, entering a cold, damp room. In front of us were three iron tables—they looked a little like old-fashioned hospital gurneys—and on top of them lay three bodies, covered to their necks with white sheets.

I was about to demand an explanation and ask again for our friends, but as I looked more closely at the figures, I realized I was looking at them: the bodies on the tables belonged to Vita, Aida and Phoenix.

SERENA
[Hazel and Tejus's daughter]

Their breathing sounded like panting, short labored breaths that made me terrified, even more so as they lay completely still, their eyes closed, their faces peaceful, as if they were asleep…or in death.

"Oh, my God," I breathed, rushing over to my brother. I felt for his hand, lifting up part of the sheet to find it. His fingers were ice-cold, and unyielding. I placed mine over them, hoping I could somehow warm him.

"What have you done!" I shouted, turning toward the monster by the door. Jovi was bent over Aida, his figure as still as the bodies on the table. *What nightmare have we entered?* I had thought this place resembled a stuffy old museum. Now it was fast becoming a house of horrors.

"Nothing," he replied sternly. "As I told you, they are experiencing a transformation—not activated by me."

I turned, ready to claw out his eyes, but Jovi beat me to it. Leaping across the room, suddenly more beast than man, he launched himself at our abductor. Jovi reached out to grasp his neck, but the man lifted his arm, slamming it into Jovi's face. I expected the werewolf to stumble back and cry out at the force of the impact, but instead Jovi flew through the air, clearing the length of the room and slamming into the furthest wall.

"Jovi!" I cried, running toward him.

He sat up as I reached him, looking furious and dazed, but not seriously injured. I turned to face the man, reaching out for him with all the mental strength I could muster. He scowled, feeling my attempts to drain him. With the force of my syphon he should have at least wavered, clutched his head in agony, or cried out. Instead, he cocked an eyebrow, almost amused at my efforts. He closed his eyes, muttering something under his breath that I couldn't hear. A split second later, he placed his palm on his forehead—gently, almost as if in prayer. I felt my link with his mind break, the tendrils of energy I'd sent out to drain him vanishing as if they were nothing but mists.

"What are you, and what's your name?" I asked, breathing heavily. My own head had started to ache furiously, drained of any mental reserves I'd had left.

"I'm a Druid," he replied evenly, "and that's what you can call me. I doubt that you have come across my kind before. We live in the In-Between, and there are too few of us left."

"Is that like a warlock?" I asked, trying to ascertain exactly how much danger we had gotten into.

"No."

I waited for him to elaborate further, but he remained silent. In frustration, I turned away from him, helping Jovi to his feet. The werewolf was almost shaking with rage.

"When will they wake up?" Jovi demanded, his jaw clenched so tightly he could hardly speak.

"That I do not know," the Druid replied. "I haven't seen the transformation take place before—this is as new to me as it is to you."

"*What* transformation?" I replied angrily. "Stop answering with riddles we don't understand! You claim you're helping them—explain to me how? Explain to me how they weren't safe on a star, surrounded by some of the most powerful supernaturals in existence?"

"If you think for a moment that 'GASP', or whatever your band of merry supernaturals call themselves," he bit out, "are more powerful than what will be coming for your friends, you are a fool."

I laughed at the Druid, so incensed by his dismissive attitude that I half felt like I'd gone completely mad. Who the *hell* did he think he was?

"You have made a huge mistake," I replied once my hysteria had calmed. "Whatever you are, whatever this place is, whatever is happening to my friends and my brother— you are going to *pay*. You obviously don't understand who you're messing with. My family will hunt you down, and they won't rest until you've been hung, drawn and quartered at their hands!"

"Enough," Jovi murmured to me, clutching my arm. I hadn't realized that my body had started to shake. "Take it easy," he continued in a soothing voice.

I looked back at the Druid, expecting a stream of anger in retaliation. Instead, something that resembled pity flickered across his expression. It was so swift I thought I had imagined it.

"I wouldn't count on it," he replied softly.

I shook my head, dismissing him. He didn't know our families. Whatever he *thought* he knew was wrong. They would come for him, and us. It was just a matter of time.

"You may remain here, with your friends, if you wish," the Druid continued. "All I ask is that you don't venture outside. It is not safe. Trust me when I say that you don't understand this world—Eritopia is deadly."

"Eritopia?" Jovi questioned.

The Druid nodded.

"The most cursed land that ever grew in these worlds," he spat. "Don't underestimate it."

And with that, he was gone.

SERENA
[HAZEL AND TEJUS'S DAUGHTER]

Still trembling, I approached the figures on the beds. I still couldn't quite relate them to my brother and friends. These still bodies terrified me, and I felt like their faces were only the masks of those I loved. This time, I stood by Vita, wanting to smooth her pale brow, but unsure if I should touch her. Their breathing still echoed around the room, the horrible, rasping pants matching my own accelerated heartbeat.

"Have you ever heard of a Druid?" Jovi asked, his voice making me jump.

"Not really… well, nothing other than human druids you read about in fairytales. You know, the kind who hang out at summer solstice wearing long beards and white robes." I tried to keep my voice as calm and reasonable as possible. I turned away from Vita and focused on Jovi.

"What do we do?" I asked quietly, hoping that the Druid wasn't able to hear us. "I don't trust him in the slightest, and the fact that I can't syphon off him makes me even more nervous."

"I know," he agreed. "At least we know we're in the In-Between. There must be fae or other species around here that we recognize. They might know Sherus and be willing to help."

I nodded, but wondered if Jovi was being overly optimistic. I recalled the conversation I'd had with Corrine—how vast the In-Between actually was, how much of it was unknown to her and any other supernaturals we knew. On the other hand, we had few options before us— it was either getting out of here, or waiting for the Druid to decide our fate.

"What about them?" I asked quietly, my fingers flitting across the sheet that covered Vita.

"I don't know," Jovi replied, raking his hair back in

frustration. He let out a growl and started pacing back and forth across the room. "I don't even know how we ended up here. The last thing I saw was you and the girls, but why is Phoenix here? He wasn't in the room, right? And where's Field? He was with us."

"I don't know," I replied. "Phoenix was in the room next to us—I know that much. But you're right, why us, why not Field?"

Jovi cursed, kicking the damp brickwork in disgust.

"I say we get out of here," he replied a moment later. "Let's see what's around at least—get our bearings. We can come back for them, once we find a way home."

I fell silent.

"I'm worried about the Druid doing something...leaving them like this—they're completely defenseless." I shook my head. Could I leave my brother here, and my friends? I wasn't sure I could.

"We don't have a choice, Serena," Jovi reminded me, his voice low. I noticed that he hadn't come near Aida since we first entered the room. He obviously couldn't bear to see her looking like this, but I also got the impression that like me, he couldn't quite get his head around the fact that the body on the table was his sister.

"We do. We can wait," I replied softly. "Wait till they come out of this…*trance*, or whatever it is."

"We don't know how long that's going to be. Or if it's a spell or something that the Druid's put them under. We don't know anything of his powers—what he might be capable of."

He was right. We had no idea whether or not this was some elaborate ruse to trap us here—for what purpose, I didn't know—and I was definitely opposed to finding out.

"Okay," I agreed. "Shall we head toward the greenhouse I saw, try to get out that way?"

Jovi nodded, trying to smile reassuringly at me, but his eyes were dulled. He glanced at Aida, and then looked away again.

"Let's get moving."

He led the way out of the room, not once looking back while I kissed each of them goodbye on the forehead—hating the feel of their cold, damp skin on my lips.

I followed Jovi back up the stairs, hoping that the Druid wouldn't be back in front of the fire, waiting for us. When Jovi reached the top of the staircase, he held out his hand to stop me. He peered through a crack in the door as I used True Sight—my vision coming out in black and white, and fuzzy, another reminder of how fast my energy was depleting. The room was clear, the chair empty. Jovi sighed with relief and we emerged into the claustrophobic heat of the room.

"Which way?" Jovi asked.

I tried to remember the layout of the house as best I could, and led him quietly from the room by the door we'd first entered. We hurried back down the hallway, past a few more empty rooms till we came to the main entrance. I paused, trying to use my True Sight again to navigate.

"I think we keep going ahead," I replied, "this way."

Hearing a noise, a sudden thump coming from upstairs, I started to run. We quickly found the entrance to the greenhouse through another door. It opened onto a small sitting room—yet another fire was lit, with the walls almost completely covered in books. The wall in front of us had been knocked through, creating a large arch covered in frosted glass. Jovi rattled the small brass handle of the door, and it flew open. We stepped inside, being careful to close it behind us.

If I'd thought the house was humid, it was nothing compared to this. The air was damp and thick with the smell of fresh soil and strongly perfumed flowers. It was also huge—dozens of feet long and wide, with only one small path not obscured by plants that led to the exit. We began to walk forward, gently pushing the wide-leafed trees out of our way, and stepping around the wide and elaborate pots that held exotic blooms in multitudes of bright colors.

"Do you think any of them are poisonous?" I asked Jovi, staring at a neon-yellow and pink flower that despite its beauty somehow managed to look venomous.

"It wouldn't surprise me," he replied.

We reached the exit, and Jovi tried the door again.

"This one's locked," he stated.

"Damn," I muttered, trying the handle again. Before I could say anything like, "Let's see if there's a key around," Jovi had whipped off his shirt and wrapped it around his fist. In one swift movement, he slammed his hand through the pane of glass. It shattered, cascading down from its frame.

"Be careful," he warned, gesturing for me to go first.

I stepped cautiously through, avoiding the sharpened points of shards still stuck in the frame. I suddenly felt ridiculous in my robe and pajamas—they were an old pair, with pink spotted pants and a lacy grey camisole top. I hoped that somewhere on our journey I'd be able to find a place to change.

Jovi emerged behind me, and we surveyed the overgrown grass of the garden and the swamps beyond. I ducked suddenly, pulling Jovi down with me as large wings flapped up above us. When I looked up, my grip on Jovi relaxed.

"We were wondering where you were." My nonchalant comment belied the total relief I felt at his sudden appearance.

Field dropped down from the sky, looking astonished to see us.

SERENA
[HAZEL AND TEJUS'S DAUGHTER]

"What are you doing here?" Field asked. "I thought I was totally alone in this house—I got out as quickly as I could." The Hawk was still dressed in his suit from the celebration, looking as rumpled as Jovi and I did. In his hands, he carried a thick vine coiled like a whip that he must have taken from the swamp trees.

Jovi shook his head, rising to his feet.

"We were all put in separate rooms," the werewolf replied. "Serena found me—the others are inside as well…but, I don't know, they're under some kind of spell."

Jovi continued to tell him about the Druid and the state of our friends, while I kept half of my attention on the house, wanting us to keep moving before the Druid made a reappearance. From outside, the house reminded me of a southern plantation, which made me wonder if we were even in the In-Between…what on earth would a building like this be doing here?

"We can't leave without them," Field announced, his aquamarine eyes flashing with unease. "I've explored the area around here; there's nothing but jungle for miles, with more swampland. There are what looks like a couple of cities way off in the distance, one east and one to the west, but I didn't want to get any closer without knowing anything about the land, or what might live here. They didn't look too welcoming either."

Before I could ask Field to elaborate on what he'd seen, I heard the approach of the Druid.

"He's coming," I said, jumping back just as the door to the greenhouse swung open. The Druid stood before us, his broad frame suddenly seeming huge and threatening as he tensed with barely concealed fury. My heart pounded in my chest as I looked at his face. The inquisitive gray eyes had gone, replaced with a black film that covered his eyes like shutters—I'd thought he was handsome before, but now he appeared terrifying, the harsh planes of his face deadly and cruel.

"I told you not to leave this place!" he shouted, moving toward Jovi and Field. Before the Druid could take another step, Field lashed out with the whip of vine, its tip cutting the chest of its intended victim and its length wrapping around him, binding his arms to his sides. The Druid laughed. I tried to run, dragging Jovi and Field with me to safety. I had only taken a step when a loud screeching almost perforated my eardrums and a huge flock of ravens descended on Field, flapping their coal-colored wings in his face, their talons outstretched.

Field fought and struggled, trying to bat them away with his own wings, but in horror I watched as they clawed at his face and head, pecking cruelly at his flesh and wings.

"Make it stop!" I cried, Jovi and I both trying to brush the birds off, but there were so many of them, all viciously intent on attacking Field. The Druid said something, a word or a phrase that I didn't quite catch, and the birds ceased—flying back up into the air and darting off behind the roof of the house.

Field was panting, his body covered in small slashes and

cuts, his suit in tatters. I looked back at the Druid, the vine lying in a pool at his feet. His eyes had returned to their normal gray, which I took as a promising sign that there was no further attack to come.

"What is *wrong* with you?" Jovi growled at the Druid. "We want answers—proper ones. I want to know what you *are*."

"Stop trying to attack me, and I'll tell you what I know," he replied, his frustration at our behavior plainly evident. It worried me that he clearly didn't see Field or Jovi as a threat—which would indicate, along with what he'd proven so far, that his abilities were stronger than ours and we were at a clear disadvantage.

"Fine," Jovi bit out, his hands raised in mock surrender. "Get on with it."

The Druid raised an eyebrow, folding his arms across his chest.

"This evening," he replied, obviously determined not to give in completely to Jovi's demands. He wanted us to know where we stood—and right now, in this land, it seemed to be at the bottom of the food chain.

"We'll have a civilized conversation," the Druid continued, "if you're capable of such a thing. If you are, I will tell you everything then. In the meantime, though it seems to have escaped your notice, your friends need assistance, which only I can provide. Bother me again by trying to leave, or conducting another fruitless attack, and I will cease in attending to them and leave you all to your fate."

Speech made, he turned and stormed back into the greenhouse.

"Follow!" he commanded.

I looked at Jovi and Field.

"It doesn't seem like we have much choice," I whispered, "not if we want answers."

"I don't like giving in," Jovi snapped.

"Neither do I," replied Field with an agitated sigh. "But we need to hear what he has to say. At least to learn a bit more about where we are before we attempt to leave again."

"All right." Jovi nodded. "He gets one chance."

We all trailed in, feeling disheartened. I didn't say anything to the others, but I actually felt relieved that we wouldn't be leaving without Phoenix and the girls. I didn't think it would be a good idea for us to be parted, even if their supposed 'transformation' was a trick.

The Druid vanished again once we entered the house.

"So, what do we do till dinner?" Jovi asked, looking around at the shabby interior with distaste.

"We explore," I replied. "All that junk upstairs—some of it's got to provide us with at least a bit of information. I want to know more about the Druids, and try to get a better understanding of what we're up against."

"He must be a type of magic-wielder, surely," Field said. "Controlling those birds like that…It's something I've only seen jinn or witches do."

"He denies he's a warlock," I replied, "and he's evidently not a jinni. I think we're dealing with a distinct species…did you see his eyes?" I asked, shuddering.

"Yeah," Jovi replied softly, taking my hand, and we walked up the stairs. His small act of reassurance was a cold comfort. I felt like we were way over our heads here—the idea that we might be stuck somewhere in the depths of the In-Between, light years away from our families and GASP, made me feel hollow and empty inside.

SERENA
[HAZEL AND TEJUS'S DAUGHTER]

All three of us headed back upstairs in search of clues.

"Wow," Field commented as we reached the hallway, "this is a lot of junk."

"Didn't you see this already?" I asked, wondering how he'd left the house in the first place.

He shook his head. "Flew out of the window."

"Right." Of course he had. Not for the first time, I envied the Hawk his natural abilities. Not to say mine weren't helpful, but they depended too much on my energy levels. What I could and couldn't do relied on how many people I could syphon and how much sleep and food I'd had.

"So, a fan of taxidermy," Field continued, picking up a moth-eaten cat. "That doesn't exactly make me warm to him."

"I don't know," I replied slowly. "This stuff is so old…what if it belonged to whoever lived here before him?"

"Whoever it was is probably buried in a basement somewhere," Jovi muttered.

I grimaced. I didn't want to think too much about the Druid and what he was capable of. "Put the cat down, Field," I snapped, leading the way to the nearest door. It opened with a creak, and we all peered inside.

It was another bedroom, a bit more lavish than mine and Jovi's had been—the floor was carpeted and a huge chandelier hung from the middle of the room, along with bookcases and a vanity table. Everything was covered in a thick layer of dust, giving the impression that the room hadn't been touched in centuries. I walked over to the vanity table, noticing an open jewelry box containing expensive gold and silver necklaces and bracelets, along with a beautiful diamond engagement ring. I didn't touch anything, but wondered who would leave all these things here, open like this, with the box unlocked. There were also old perfume bottles, still containing liquids, and a crystal powder-holder, yellowed with age. I started to seriously consider the fate of whoever had lived here before the Druid. Had they been killed? Had they been human or supernatural?

"Come on, there's nothing in here. Let's try somewhere else." Jovi and Field returned to the doorway.

"Serena?" Jovi prompted.

"Coming," I replied. "Just go next door—I'll follow you in a second."

As they left, I pulled open the drawer beneath the dresser. It was bare apart from a thick, leather-bound notebook. I flicked through the pages, my eyes widening as I saw neat but cramped handwriting filling each of the pages—I was looking at someone's journal. My immediate reaction was to return it to where I'd found it. Prying into someone's most personal, most intimate thoughts wasn't okay, even if I suspected that person to be long dead. I hesitated before putting it back in the drawer.

What if it holds answers?

"Serena!" Jovi called, startling me.

I dropped the diary back in the drawer, shutting it hastily.

"Sorry," I replied, joining them in the next room. I instantly realized that we'd hit the jackpot. The room we'd entered was small, and every available surface was covered in shelves with cardboard and metal cylinders. In the middle of the room was a desk, covered with a large, hand-drawn map.

Jovi and Field were poring over it, and I joined them, my interest spiking even further as I read the inscription on the top of the map, labeled 'Eritopia'.

"Here we are, I think." Field pointed out to a mark on the map, labeled 'Wolstone House,' with a small, architecturally correct layout of the building we were in. I could even see the greenhouse, and the markings of where the lawn ended and the swamps began. I looked to see what surrounded us, which was mostly as I'd seen—swamps, more swamps and then jungle.

"'Storm Hounds,'" Jovi read out, pointing at small markings that were dotted along the swamps. "That doesn't sound too good—what are storm hounds?"

"Not sure I want to know," I murmured.

I focused my attentions on the two cities, or villages, marked out on the map—one to the east and one to the west, just as Field had mentioned. They didn't look very large, but each was surrounded by rings marked in red ink.

"Does that mean danger or something?" Jovi asked, tracing his finger along the lines.

"Or it's where a territory has been reduced," Field remarked. "Maybe the cities were once much larger than they are now."

"There are no pathways shown," noted Jovi. "When we leave, we'll have to cross through the jungle for miles before we reach any kind of civilization."

"And we don't know how safe they are," Field remarked. "What I saw were walled cities—I could hardly see inside them. Like I said, not inviting."

"Well, if this area's as dangerous as the Druid said it is, maybe that's not surprising. We don't know what they're trying to keep out," I replied.

"Maybe they're keeping out the Druid," Jovi speculated.

"All that for one Druid?" I asked—it didn't seem likely to me. He might have been powerful, but walls so high that even Field hadn't been able to see into them seemed a bit like overkill.

"Don't underestimate him," Field warned me. "We don't know anything yet—let's make sure we stay on guard."

"He knows a lot about us," Jovi mused. "I mean, if it's so dangerous to leave the house, how did he get to us? He knew what GASP was, knew about our kind—he knew I was a werewolf, and didn't seem surprised by your presence." He turned to Field. "He's way ahead of us."

"Then that's something we need to remedy," Field replied. "Start checking all the maps. What we need is a bigger one, one that will show us where we are in relation to the fae stars."

I started pulling down the largest maps I could see, sliding their heavy paper out of the cylindrical containers and laying them down flat wherever there was space. Many of them were useless, either replicas of the one we'd just found, or of entirely different places, their annotations written in languages I couldn't understand. We even found a few of Earth—America, Africa, Europe—old maps that must have been from centuries ago, detailing countries with old names that were no longer in existence.

"I think we have to assume that whoever lived here before was just a collector," I stated eventually, feeling like I'd looked at hundreds of maps that were no use to us whatsoever. The sky was also darkening. We'd opened a window to let in some air—not that it helped much since it was so humid. The sky was red and gold, the sun setting rapidly, leaving the swamps covered in darkness, and only the tips of the mountains and highest reaches of the jungle were still bathed in light.

"When do you think we go down for dinner?" Jovi asked, following my gaze out of the window.

"Not sure. Maybe we'll be called?" I speculated.

Both of them looked at me.

"What?" I replied. "He seems old-fashioned, don't you think? Inviting us to 'dine' with him—it seems like whatever he is, he's also under the pretense of being a gentleman."

Jovi guffawed. "A gentleman? I'm leaning toward serial killer if anything," he replied, looking at me in disbelief.

"I actually think Serena's right," Field added. "I think if we join him tonight, and try to keep our manners in check"—he looked pointedly at Jovi—"then we might get some of the answers we need."

"I think Serena's our best bet on that," Jovi argued.

"What do you mean?" I asked, genuinely confused.

"Druid or not, he's still a man, and I don't think he's immune to…you know, your *charm*," he teased.

"Oh, knock it off," I replied, rolling my eyes. "Field's

right. We eat with him, we ask questions, we try to be polite, and then we get our friends and get out of here. There will be no femme fatale part of the plan—we're not in a spy movie, Jovi."

He shrugged. "Whatever… I still think you should lead the questions."

"I'm happy to do that," I retorted, "but more because of my budding journalism skills than anything else. I'm going to have a shower before we go down—I'm covered in dust and boiling hot. See you all downstairs?"

"No," Jovi corrected, "see you at the top of the staircase—we go down together."

"Fine," I replied, "see you shortly."

I left the room, already looking forward to a cold shower. I wished I had something to wear other than my pajamas though—not only did I feel embarrassingly underdressed for when we left the house to trek though miles of jungle, but my clothes were also filthy and covered in a layer of dust and grime that would make me feel instantly dirty again the moment I got clean.

As I walked to my room, I kept my eyes averted from the stuffed animals and the grotesque ceiling. I thought about what Jovi had said, about the Druid noticing my 'charms'—I kind of wanted to punch Jovi for making a comment like that, but I also wondered how true it was. I recalled the way the Druid had stared at my hand clasped in Jovi's, and how uncomfortable that had made me feel…I wasn't really sure why.

SERENA
[HAZEL AND TEJUS'S DAUGHTER]

I re-entered the room I'd been in when I arrived and checked the door on the other side of the room, correctly guessing that it was a bathroom. I sighed with relief when I noticed a small copper bath and an old-fashioned shower head. The tub was full of cobwebs, but there was an old, only slightly moth-eaten towel hanging on the back of the door. I tried the taps first, not worried if there wasn't any hot water—I would definitely only be using cold. To my surprise, after a short gurgling of pipes, the water flowed from the showerhead forcefully, and there was both hot and cold water available. Next I searched under the sink for some soap, finding a thick block of it wrapped in rotting tissue paper.

I gave the tub a rinse and then stepped under the faucet, reveling in the feeling of the water beating against my skin. I closed my eyes, trying not to picture Phoenix and my friends lying on those eerie-looking hospital beds, but it was an image that hadn't really left my mind since I'd first seen them—no matter how hard I'd tried to focus on getting out of here.

I used the bar of soap to clean myself, even using it on my hair, whilst vainly wishing for Corrine's herbal concoction back in The Shade. Once I was satisfied, I stepped out, grimacing as I used the towel. It smelt of mold, but it wasn't as bad as when I later put my pajamas back on, discarding the robe. They were filthy. Feeling like the entire shower process had been a bit of a waste of time, I stepped back into the bedroom, opening the nearest window and catching the last of the sun's rays before it dipped down completely. I looked around the room for a lamp, noticing one by the table. It was another oil lamp, with a set of damp matches next to it—but a significant amount of kerosene remained in the base. After a few tries, I finally got one of the matches to light and held the flame to the wick. It lit, casting the room in a yellow glow.

I wondered, not for the first time, how these old-fashioned human-looking objects happened to be in the depths of the In-Between. Everything I'd seen so far looked like it was straight out of the eighteen hundreds…how had it gotten here? Perhaps another question for our taciturn kidnapper this evening.

Leaving my room, I made my way back along the hallway to the staircase. I couldn't hear any sign of Field or Jovi, and was too tired to use True Sight to find their location. It also wasn't a good idea to do that while people were getting dressed…

While I waited, I noticed a large velvet curtain covering the far end of the hallway wall. I must have missed it when Jovi and I were looking around, and with all the junk surrounding it, I could see why. Now I was curious, and walked up to it, tugging at one end to pull it across. Behind it was another painting, just as gruesome as the ones on the ceiling, perhaps more so.

The painting was in oil like the others, and it depicted a single image—a demonic creature, riding on the back of a black-winged horse. The creature was half man, half snake, its tail wound around the body of the horse, squeezing its middle so the horse appeared to be silently screaming in pain. The upper part of the snake was a man—pale-skinned, muscular and broad, with a long spear in its hand, the tip painted purple, as if some venom was dripping off it. The eyes of the demon were scratched off, as if someone couldn't bear to see the no doubt deadly gaze of the beast. I shut the curtain.

No wonder someone had wanted that covered.

Turning back to the staircase, I began to grow impatient. I wanted to see my brother and friends, to check that they were okay. I tried to listen out for Field and Jovi, becoming further irritated when I heard the sounds of a shower running. They must have remained in the map room for a while after I'd left. Not willing to wait, I grabbed a book from one of the nearest piles and tore out the first page. I looked around for something to write with, but, finding nothing, I made my way back to the map room, where I'd seen pencils standing in a pot.

I scrawled quickly on the piece of paper:

'Gone down to see the others. Meet me there. Sorry. Serena.'

I hurried back to the staircase and left the paper on the

banister where they'd see it. Satisfied, I descended the stairs, being careful to avoid the weakened wood. When I reached the main entrance, I found my way back to the room where we'd first come across the Druid. The door was shut. I used True Sight to see if he was there, but couldn't make anything out—I was near useless now, and either the food this evening was going to need to be packed with protein, or I'd need to ask one of the boys if they could help me out.

The door was unlocked, so I stepped into the room, staring aghast at the still roaring fire. What was this Druid's deal? The room was hotter than hell, and I quickly made my way to the opposite door and descended the staircase, sighing in relief as the cool, damp air relieved the torture.

I paused in the doorway, partly relieved to see that they were still there, and partly dismayed. The panting was still as aggressive as it had been earlier, and I wondered if it was because they were in some kind of pain—locked in their bodies somehow so they couldn't escape. I walked over to my brother first and felt his forehead. It wasn't as damp as it had been earlier, which I guessed might have been a sign of improvement. I moved over to Aida, and then lastly to Vita. All of them felt less damp and cold, but other than that they were unchanged. Not knowing what else to do, I started to explore the rest of the room, but I couldn't find much—just a few empty drawers, and more bookshelves that were devoid of any reading material.

I jumped as someone cleared their throat behind me. It was the Druid, standing in the doorway, his gray eyes gazing at me intently.

"Sorry," I muttered, instantly irritated at myself for apologizing.

"Dinner is ready," he replied.

I nodded, swallowing. He stood to one side of the doorway, gesturing that I leave first. With a final glance at my friends, I walked to the exit and made my way up the stairs. I felt unsettled as I walked, feeling the Druid watching me as I ascended.

Serena
[Hazel and Tejus's daughter]

The Druid took the lead once we reached the ground floor. I followed him, eventually arriving in a large room that Jovi and I hadn't seen when we'd explored earlier. Field and Jovi were standing by a heavily adorned banquet table, both of them frowning at me.

"We told you to wait, Serena," Jovi said to me, ignoring the Druid completely.

"I'm sorry," I replied. "I wanted to see them."

"How are they?" Field asked.

"The same. They don't feel as cold as they did

earlier…but I don't know, that might be my imagination."

"It's not," the Druid cut in. "Their temperature should start returning to normal now. I think the worst of it is over."

"I thought you'd never seen this before," Jovi shot back, frowning at the Druid.

"From what I have read," he replied tersely, "that is what to expect."

I gave Jovi a look of warning. We needed to keep the Druid placated if we wanted any of our questions answered. Jovi nodded stiffly, pulling back a chair to sit down. The Druid watched him, and after a few moments took a seat at the far end of the table.

I took a proper look at what had been put before us. There were about nine settings made, all with glasses, cutlery, and a plate covered with a silver warming dish. Were we being joined by others? I silently took my seat, glancing down at where the Druid sat. There was no food placed before him, only a single glass filled with water.

"Eat," the Druid commanded, gesturing to the plates in front of us. I removed the dish warmer, quietly praying that whatever was beneath it would be edible. I was pleasantly surprised. The food smelt good—there was a husk of corn, a substantial-looking brown grain dish, and some strange grass shoots that looked like they'd been steamed. I picked up my fork.

"Wait," Jovi called out. I looked up, startled. He turned to the Druid. "Why aren't you eating?" he asked.

"I've already eaten," the Druid replied calmly. "I suppose you think the food is poisoned?"

"Are you surprised?" Jovi retorted.

The Druid sighed and rose from his chair. He made his way toward me and I thought he was going to stop, but he continued, reaching Field's chair.

"May I?" the Druid asked, picking up Field's fork.

"Go ahead," Field replied, crossing his arms and leaning back from the table.

The Druid speared a grass shoot, and then, turning to face Jovi, he placed it in his mouth, chewing with deliberate slowness till he had finished. He handed the fork back to Field, and then returned to his seat.

"Satisfied?" he asked, glaring at us all.

I nodded, picking up my own fork and giving Jovi another warning look. He muttered something under his breath, but proceeded to eat. I joined him, but started to grow increasingly uncomfortable as the Druid's gaze lingered on me.

"So, questions," I said, putting down my cutlery.

The Druid eyed me with amusement, leaning back and gazing at me as if in challenge.

"First, tell us about this 'transformation'. What *exactly* is happening to our friends?" I asked, determined not to be put off by his amusement. If he thought all this was funny, then good for him—but I was absolutely terrified for my friends, and failed to see how he could treat it as some kind of game or joke.

"Right to the heart of the matter," he conceded, the smile vanishing from his face. "I will get to your question, but let me tell it in my own way, as I think you will understand me better." He paused as if waiting for one of us to say something. "May I?" he asked.

"You *may*," I replied slowly, wondering why he was suddenly so accommodating. "As long as it gets to the point," I clarified.

He nodded, and I glanced at Field and Jovi—both of them were leaning forward, food forgotten as they waited for the Druid to speak.

"A while ago, some years now, my father and I were visited by an Oracle. She was known to only a few Druids, and that was mostly by myth. Most of us hardly believed that the stories were true. Her story was known to us all… she was born of an Ancient and a jinni, and her parents had hidden her long ago in a land that was far from here."

At this, I glanced over at Jovi and Field. He must be talking about the same Oracle who had lived in Nevertide and visited us in The Shade, the supposed 'fairy godmother' of my brother and friends. Jovi met my eye and subtly shook his head, warning me not to say anything. I glanced over at the Druid, but he hadn't noticed us. He looked deep in thought, as if he'd almost forgotten he had an audience.

"She came to my father and me," he continued, "begging help. She wanted us to protect her from Azazel and his creatures. We agreed, of course. My father and I have sworn to always protect the Oracle from harm."

"Who's Azazel?" I asked. I'd never heard the name before.

The Druid's gaze flickered in my direction, and he seemed mildly surprised at the question, frowning as he replied, as if the mere name was distasteful to him. "Azazel is the self-proclaimed ruler of this land—of Eritopia. To maintain his rule, he desires all power and knowledge, and to obtain this he uses the Oracles. Their powers allow him to know when harm might come his way, or any who plot against him, and he can destroy it before it comes to pass."

"And he wanted this Oracle, I take it? The one who visited you?" I clarified.

"Exactly," he murmured. "The moment she left the protections of Nevertide, she was seen—the Oracle he already had in his service saw her coming to Eritopia the moment she entered your 'Shade', and told Azazel of her presence."

I was surprised by the involvement of another Oracle. First, that there was more than one of these freaks of nature alive, and secondly, wasn't there loyalty between the species? It seemed cruel to sell out another of their kind that way. The Druid saw my look of surprise, and shook his head.

"Don't judge too harshly—the Oracles live for a long time, and Azazel is viciously cruel. We don't know what he might have promised her in return for the information, or what he might have done to get it out of her. Once an Oracle is in Azazel's hands, there is no escape."

"So what happened?" I asked, urging him on. It was starting to become obvious, from the absence of both the Druid's father and the Oracle, that this story didn't have a happy ending.

"By the time the Oracle reached us, she knew already that it was too late. Unable to communicate with us in time, she landed some distance away, outside the safety of our home. My father and I went to collect her, arriving moments before Azazel and his creatures. My father battled him, throwing me out of sight so that I might live. Her last words to me and my father were about your friends."

The Druid glanced at us all in turn. He seemed reluctant to continue his story, and anxiety knotted in my stomach.

"Please go on," I murmured, unable to stand the silence a second longer.

"She told us that she had passed on the gift of her abilities, meaning for it to be an act of kindness to the children of The Shade, so that King Derek might be able to protect your home for centuries to come. At that point, she had not been able to see what was coming—her mother, an Ancient, had kept certain visions from her, essentially blinding her to the existence of Eritopia so she did not go seeking answers or move from her safe haven in Nevertide. Her last wish was that the children of The Shade she had imparted her gifts to were to be brought here—away from Azazel's reach, able to live safely, even if it was not happily."

A stunned silence settled over us all. My mind reeled as I tried to understand what this meant for my brother and friends.

"Let me get this straight." I spoke slowly, trying to focus against the rush of white noise that was running through my head. "Phoenix, Vita, Aida—they're all going through a transformation that will result in them becoming *Oracles*?"

The Druid nodded. I looked over at Field and Jovi. Jovi was staring at the Druid like he wanted to physically harm him, his fork gripped in his hand like a weapon. Field had paled, staring at some point in the distance in disbelief.

"Sorry, how is that even *possible*?" I asked. Oracles were only born when a jinni and a witch bred together—there was no other way one of them could be created, as far as I understood. They were almost an accident, a biological supernatural twist that occurred so rarely that I had thought only one existed after the twins, Hortencia and Pythia, killed themselves by jumping into a volcano, way before I was born.

"It wouldn't be possible under normal circumstances." The Druid smirked dryly at his use of 'normal' and continued, "But your Oracle was a daughter of an Ancient, far more powerful than any that have gone before her, and any that will come after. She was able to pass on her gift somehow, and have it awaken when she willed it."

"What? You mean she *made* this happen? Why couldn't she let it stay dormant, so they'd be safe?" I was on the verge of screaming, willing to forgive the Oracle for passing on a gift she didn't know was dangerous, but certainly not for activating it!

The Druid sighed, leaning forward in his chair and looking directly at me.

"We have to trust that it was done at the right time, and for the right reasons. Perhaps it *had* to happen—maybe the gift couldn't stay dormant forever, I don't know. And we will never know… not while Azazel keeps her."

"This is ridiculous!" Jovi slammed his fists down against the table and glared at the Druid. "The twin Oracle sisters never faced a threat from whatever this man is, this *Azazel,* when they inhabited Earth—my sister and our friends would be just as fine in The Shade. If the threat is real, which, by the way, I'm still not fully convinced of, GASP could keep them far safer than you could."

"The two women you speak of committed suicide," the Druid replied calmly, unruffled by Jovi's outburst. "They saw that he was coming. They knew their time was up, and so rather than be taken by him, they did what they believed was best."

"And you know that how?" I asked. That wasn't the story Benjamin had told us of how those twins had died… unless those twins had kept the real reason of their suicide from him.

"It was seen by another," the Druid replied vaguely.

"Another Oracle?"

"Yes."

His face darkened suddenly, almost as if a shadow had crossed it. I wondered if it was sorrow—had *another* Oracle been taken from here, or been lost to him and his father, before the Nevertide Oracle's arrival in the In-Between? Before I could ask, Field interrupted.

"I want to know why you care," he said, his voice matching the calm of the Druid. "What are our friends to you? Why are you so intent on helping the Nevertide Oracle, so much so that your father apparently lost his life trying to save her?"

"My kind once ruled Eritopia—happily and fairly. If Azazel no longer holds the power of the Oracles, we may find a way to end his rule," the Druid replied. He rocked in his chair, turning his attention back to me. "That is enough questions for tonight. You can ask more tomorrow, but for now I need to return to your friends."

"Do you know any more about when they might wake?" I asked quickly, ignoring his statement.

"No."

He rose from the table, and without another word he left the room.

"I'm not sure I believe any of this," Jovi announced the moment he had gone.

"I'm not convinced either—or at least, I'm struggling to fully understand it. But I don't think we have much choice right now but to wait until they come out of the transformation," Field replied. "Serena… what do you think?"

"I don't know," I replied honestly. "He has a lot of information about us—about the Oracle twins, about the Nevertide Oracle. She did bless the trio, or do *something,* that much we know. What if it is all true?"

The consequences of that, if everything the Druid had said was true, were mind-blowing. Not only would my brother and friends become Oracles once they woke—with powers that were completely life-altering, and potentially damaging—but they would also be in grave danger… We all would.

SERENA
[HAZEL AND TEJUS'S DAUGHTER]

After the Druid left, we sat around the table in silence. My food lay half-eaten and forgotten on my plate. I tried not to picture my older brother, lying on that cold table-top, waiting for some supernatural transformation to take its effect. What would he be like when he woke up? The Druid had told us nothing about what it might be like—if he would be *blind*, for goodness' sake! I looked over at Field and Jovi…were they worrying about the same things?

"We should try to get some rest," Field said.

Rest? It was the last thing I felt like doing.

"How can we *sleep*?" I replied.

Jovi looked as surprised as I felt. Field looked pointedly at me.

"You need rest, Serena, you're fading—fast."

I shook my head. "I don't care about that. I want…" I trailed off. What did I want? For none of this to be happening. That was what I wanted, and that was the one thing that wasn't an option.

"Do you need to syphon, Serena?" Jovi asked.

"Tomorrow," I replied, "not now. I've eaten a bit, I can wait."

"Bed," Field repeated. "We all need some rest. Tomorrow we can think about all this with fresh perspective."

I raised an eyebrow at Field.

"And you?" I asked. He, like the rest of the Hawk boys, never needed much sleep—and he often slept outdoors.

"I'll be on the roof. But I'll be close, okay?" he replied.

"Okay," I said, rising from the table. "I guess we rest then."

I waited for the other two at the doorway, much less willing to move around the house alone now that it was night-time. They got up from the table, Jovi moving like he was in a daze. I took his arm and squeezed, hoping to offer him whatever small bit of comfort I could. He smiled dully at me, and we all made our way through the main entrance and then ascended the staircase.

"Call if you need anything." Jovi turned to me as we moved to part ways, the boys moving toward the right of the hallway, and me to the left.

"I will. I'll see you both in the morning."

I dragged my body along to my allocated room, the tiredness suddenly hitting me. I guessed the time difference here was taking its toll. It had been the middle of the night when the Druid had taken us from the fire star, and so I'd lost out on a full night's sleep. I pushed open the door to my room, hating the pitch darkness that met me. I felt around for the lamp by the side of the bed, which had gone out since I left, and then blindly hunted for the matches. After a few mistaken fumbles, I got the wick lit and the room was suffused with yellow light.

I opened both windows as wide as they could go. It didn't make much difference to the temperature of the room, but at least it would make it smell less musty. Leaning out, I could hear the ropes of moss moving gently in the branches with what small amount of breeze there was, and the hush of what sounded like cricket calls. The latter was reassuring just because it was familiar to me.

I sat on the bed, wondering how I was going to sleep with my head whirring the way it was and the blanket of heat that was drenching me in perspiration. I decided to take another shower, carrying the lamp into the bathroom with me and placing it down at a safe distance from the water.

When I was clean, I wrapped myself in the towel, dreading putting on my pajamas, which, quite frankly, were starting to seriously smell. I walked back to the wardrobe, pulling open the doors. It was empty as I recalled, but this time I noticed a single drawer beneath and tugged it open. The moldy scent was unpleasant, but I found neatly folded fabrics, and started to pull them out one by one, hoping there might be something I could wear in bed.

I found some bed-sheets, the same off-white ones that were currently covering the bed, an old woolen shawl that had seen better days, and then, at the bottom of the pile, two white nightdresses—once again, about as old-fashioned as possible, with long white sleeves with lace cuffs and a high, frilly collar. Under any other circumstances, I would have laughed at the thought of wearing something as ridiculous as this. I suddenly found myself missing Aida and

Vita so much it made my heart hurt. I just wanted them to wake up—wake up and be perfectly fine, and exactly the same as they always had been, so they could laugh at me in this stupid nightgown.

After getting dressed, I started to wash my pajamas in the shower. They could dry overnight, and at least they'd be clean.

Once that was done, I started to pace the room. I was too shaken to sleep, and half contemplating the idea of going to see if Jovi was still awake, but I couldn't hear any other sounds coming from the house. Either he'd managed to sleep, or he was at least trying to.

Do the same, idiot. Get some rest.

I placed the lamp next to the bed and shoved the sheets aside. Gingerly I climbed in, hating the smell of mildew and damp that wafted off the bedding. I lay back, staring up at the ceiling and unwilling to blow out the light.

My body felt exhausted, and it sank into the mattress gratefully, but my mind was tuned into every slight sound—every creak of plumbing or groan of the old house. It kept me irritatingly alert, my adrenaline spiking every time I heard a noise that sounded unfamiliar to me.

"Serena...Serena."

I sat bolt upright in bed.

What was that?

I listened for the sound again, my heartbeat running at such a rapid and loud pace that I had trouble hearing anything else.

"Serena." The call came again from outside the window. It sounded more like a whisper, called out in a tense, anguished voice... could that be the boys? I ran over and peered out into the garden. In the moonlight, I could make out two figures at the far end of the lawn.

What are they doing?

"Serena, come on," they called again urgently, and this time I distinctly placed it as Field's voice. I was instantly angry—whatever they were doing, we should have gone downstairs together!

"What are you doing?" I called out as loudly as I dared.

"Just get down here. We'll explain!" Jovi shot back.

Ugh. "Okay, I'm coming!" I hissed, and waved at them both, indicating that I was coming down. I picked up the lamp from the bedside table and hurried out of the door. I ran as quietly as I could along the hallway, keeping my footsteps light and avoiding looking at any of the disturbing artifacts that had freaked me out earlier.

When I reached the staircase, I moved more slowly, avoiding the crack and wincing at every creak in the wood. I headed straight for the greenhouse, hoping that the Druid hadn't had time to fix the glass pane. When I entered the tropical heat of the room, I was relieved to find that the exit was still open, and I picked my way gingerly across the glass-covered floor. I placed the lamp down by the exit and then stepped out onto the lawn.

I sighed with relief when I saw that they were still waiting for me—they hadn't moved from their position at the edge of the lawn. I hurried into the overgrown grass, wondering if this was a stupid idea. The Druid had said that leaving the grounds was close to suicide…was it really something we wanted to be doing in the middle of the night?

"Serena, come on." The voice came again, this time sounding more like Field.

"Yeah, I'm *coming*," I replied angrily. As I ran across the lawn, the grass whipped at the nightdress and my bare feet, highlighting just how badly I was dressed for an escape plan—or whatever the heck this was.

The lawn was larger than it looked from above, and it seemed to take forever for me to reach them. They kept waiting patiently for me, not moving, and I wondered why

Field wasn't at least helping me out a bit by coming to pick me up. At the halfway point between the house and my friends, I heard the flutter of wings. Thinking that Field had finally got his act together, I looked up expectantly. It wasn't Field, it was a bunch of ravens, circling me and squawking loudly.

"Go away!" I hissed at them, picking up my pace. Instead of backing off, they started to fly around my head—not pecking at me, but smacking their large wings into my face and leaving me disorientated. I threw my hands up, trying to knock them back, but they continued to circle me rapidly, their cries loud in my ears as they blocked out the moonlight and all I could feel was their thick feathers bashing into my face and limbs.

"Get off!" I cried.

"Serena, come on," the boys called out again.

This time I lost my temper. Summoning up my energy as best I could, and focusing it on the crying birds, I tried to manipulate them through syphoning—telling them to leave me alone while simultaneously trying to drain their energy so they'd back off. It was a skill that was underdeveloped in me, and I wasn't sure how well it would work. To my surprise, I felt myself connecting with the creatures, sensing their strange, hysterical panic. The syphoning disorientated them, and I took my chance, racing ahead to meet the boys at the other end of the lawn.

"Thanks for the help!" I called out, panting as I ran.

The moment I got within a few paces of them, I watched in utter disbelief as they turned and started running into the swamplands.

"Are you kidding me?" I cried out, coming to a standstill.

"We'll explain!" Jovi hissed. "We just need to get a bit further from the house."

His tone was the same urgent call I'd heard earlier, and it sent a rush of goosebumps up the back of my neck. What had they discovered?

"Serena," Field called out, his voice fast fading as they ran on ahead.

As dumb as this idea seemed, I didn't want to be left here on my own. I started to rush through the swamplands, my bare feet slapping against soggy soil. I stuck to the areas where the trees grew, not wanting to sink into water. There was just enough moonlight to guide me, and I could make out their shadowy figures up ahead.

As I ran, I resolved to talk some sense into them when I finally caught up with them. I was beyond angry, and in the past, would never for a moment have even *thought* that either of them would behave this way.

"Can you wait up?" I cried out, almost stumbling on a vine that caught around my ankle. I paused to untangle myself, and when I looked up again, they had gone.

"Jovi? Field?" I called out.

My voice sounded hollow and echoed across the silent swamp. The crickets had stopped, and now there was just an airless silence that sank into my bones.

"Jovi?" I called again, hating the sound of my voice—timid and alone.

I moved forward, brushing aside a curtain of willow boughs. The moonlight shone down on a small island rise in the swamp. Field and Jovi were standing still, watching me. I couldn't make out their features properly—their eyes were cast in shadow, their figures not looking… quite right.

"Guys?" I stammered. "What…What's going on?"

They didn't say anything, just continued to watch me. My body screamed out for me to stop moving—to turn around and run back as fast as I could toward the house. My mind tried to act rationally, moving my body forward. They were waiting for me, that was all.

They're not my friends.

The thought came as a whisper through my mind, and I stopped moving. My limbs froze in complete terror. Field smiled at me, and it was all wrong.

SERENA
[HAZEL AND TEJUS'S DAUGHTER]

I heard a shrill cry to my left, up in the trees. I looked up, seeing a black figure jumping from one tree to another. It moved on its hands and feet, giving the impression of something that was almost human, but not quite. I stumbled back, my eyes shifting in horror to where Field and Jovi had stood. They'd vanished.

Before I could turn and run, there was another ear-splitting cry to my right. It sounded like a child screaming—a wail that was desperate, hungry. More figures, all moving on four legs, jumped from the trees. The boughs shook, and I could hear the soft thumps as they landed. This time I turned and started to move across the swampland, jumping to the small patches of land.

Another cry went up, closer this time, almost as it if was right behind me. I turned, silently screaming as a pair of fangs—large, and shining a brilliant white in the light of the moon—snapped next to my face. I could smell the putrid breath of the creature, like rotted meat, hot on my skin. In a split second it was gone, and the black figure jumped onto another branch.

I had been tricked—whatever these creatures were, they had lured me into the depths of the swamp to trap me. I started running again, my breath coming out in harsh pants as I dodged the roots of the trees in the soil, praying not to stumble. If I did, that would be it.

I could hear them easily keeping pace with my strides. They screamed down at me from the trees and splashed in the water behind me, some of them running through the water as they gained on me. I kept running in a straight line, heading to where I could just about see the house in the distance. Leaping over a wide stretch of water, I landed clumsily on the other side. I stumbled, just for a moment, and one of the creatures dropped down in front of me.

Its jaws opened in another shriek, its body crouched low on the ground, two arms in front of it, knuckles grazing on the earth, with its hind legs ready to leap up toward me. I couldn't see the creature's eyes—its face seemed to be entirely composed of jaw and muscle, attached to an almost bare skull, hairless like the rest of its body.

This time I screamed, dodging to the left and falling into a pool of water. I sent out a barrier of energy, trying to create a dome around myself that would block them. As soon as the barrier took form I realized it wouldn't be enough—my mind was disordered and weak, too panicked to create anything that might save me. I scrambled to my feet, running on through the water to the nearest ground.

I heard their cries start up again, and the softer movements of them leaping up into the trees. They were enjoying the chase, toying with me, when I knew they could attack and kill me at any moment. I kept running on, seeing the edge of the swamp. Another howl came at me from the left, and I veered off the path to get away from it. I took another leap, but this time was yanked back—something had caught on my nightgown. I turned around, trying to pull it free at the same time. It was caught in the claws of one of them, and the creature yanked it back, swinging me around to face the others.

They had all crouched low in a semi-circle, as if patiently waiting for some signal to leap forward. Their cries had stopped, and all I could hear was my own panting and my heartbeat thudding in my chest. I spun around, back in the direction of the house, but silently, so silently I hadn't heard a thing, more of them had crept around the back. They were crouched low too—waiting, watching.

I was completely surrounded.

Trying to focus my energy and adrenaline, I threw a barrier as forcefully as I could in the direction of the creatures that blocked the way to the house. It sent two of them reeling back, screeching again, excited that I was putting up a fight. I took my chance—running as fast as I could in the gap they'd left. They gave chase again. Branches whipped at my face and reeds at my legs, but I could barely feel the slices they were gouging into my skin.

Hardly looking where I was going, just praying that I could keep moving until I reached the lawn, I slammed into something hard and solid. Staggering back, I looked up to see the black eyes of the Druid.

SERENA
[HAZEL AND TEJUS'S DAUGHTER]

Shoving me aside, he threw a flurry of knives into the air—slim blades making contact with the ground and some of the tree trunks with heavy thuds. A split second after the knives had landed, flames flew up in their place, burning blue and silver as if the metal itself had ignited.

The creatures scurried to the tops of the trees that weren't burning, screaming down at us—their jaws gnashing at the night's air, running heavily with saliva. I watched in horror as one of them brushed past one of the flames, its body instantly becoming engulfed in the blue fire. It reared up on its hind legs, toppling backward, looking like a human being burned alive.

I turned my face away, ready to run, my legs shaking so much I didn't know if I could move them. Without a word, the Druid lifted me roughly up into his arms as if I was no heavier than a feather, and started to run in the direction of the house. I tried to resist, insisting that I could run on my own, but he didn't seem to be listening to a word I said.

Cradled the way I was, I could see behind the Druid to the beasts that we'd left behind. The fires had started to die down, the creatures once again following us with their cries and howls of anguish at being denied their meal. Unthinkingly, I clutched at the Druid's arms, my nails pressing into his clothing. I could see them gaining on us rapidly, and I cried out in alarm, wanting to warn him.

Suddenly the Druid leapt over one of the islands, skidding to a halt.

"What are you doing?" I yelled, needing him to keep moving. He didn't reply, but started to march forward at a slower pace. Three of the creatures leapt toward us, and I tried to wriggle my way free of the Druid's grasp, but he held on, his grip like stone. Helpless, and wild-eyed with horror, I watched the creatures leap in mid-air—before being knocked back into the swamp water with a heavy splash.

"They can't cross," the Druid muttered without breaking his stride. The howls continued as the creatures clawed at the thin air but were unable to cross over.

"Is it a barrier?" I asked breathlessly, my chest heaving as I fought to control my breath.

"Something like that," he replied.

"Serena!"

A shout went up, and I turned my head to see Jovi and Field moving toward us—Jovi running, and Field with his wings outstretched, flying low across the grass of the lawn. Before they could reach us, the Druid barked at them, "Inside!" without relinquishing his pace or his grip on me.

"What did you do to her?" Jovi cried angrily.

I tried to shake my head to indicate that this time the Druid had saved my life, but I was too jittery to speak, the adrenaline slowly leaving my body. I started to tremble all over, feeling weak and completely devoid of any energy. As we moved across the grounds, Field and Jovi matching the Druid's pace while they looked at me with shock and concern, I felt glad that I didn't have to stand or walk—my body felt incapable of doing either.

"You can put her down now," Jovi told the Druid tersely as we reached the greenhouse. He was ignored, and the Druid only shifted me in his arms as he navigated the glassless door.

"Someone pick up the light," the Druid snapped as we entered.

Field picked it up, and the two of them followed us into the sitting room just beyond the greenhouse. The Druid placed me down in an armchair, in front of an empty fireplace. As he released me, I realized that he was trembling with rage. I was also dimly aware that I suddenly felt cold, my body noticing the absence of the Druid's warmth more than anything else.

"Are you okay?" Jovi crouched down next to the chair, and I nodded numbly at him.

"What happened?" he asked, reaching down to my arms to hold them. I noticed I was still shaking, and tried to force myself to stop, but my body just wouldn't comply.

"I heard you calling," I replied, my brain feeling fuzzy as I tried to piece together the bits of the story. "The creatures, whatever they were, sounded just like you and Field. And they *looked* like you...until they changed."

"What?" Jovi and Field replied together, astonishment

coloring their tone.

"They're shape-shifters," the Druid interjected, throwing logs onto the fire and not looking in our direction. "Not ones any of you would be familiar with. Once they see and hear a creature, human or supernatural, they can take on its appearance and voice almost perfectly. They must have heard you when you were outside earlier today. Many creatures have met their end by following what they perceive to be friends or loved ones into jungles and swamps, finding themselves surrounded before they realize they've been tricked."

"You didn't think to tell us about these creatures?" Jovi shot back, glaring at the Druid. The fire leapt to life, casting his face in the light of the red flame.

"I told you it was dangerous out there. I *told* you not to leave the land—they are not the worst things out there, not by any stretch of the imagination. Serena was lucky."

Lucky?

I felt grateful to be alive and unharmed, but I certainly didn't consider myself lucky.

"Do you want to go upstairs, Serena?" Field asked, his eyes wide with concern.

"I'm okay here for a moment… just need to catch my

breath."

I felt comforted by the heat of the fire. The night was still warm, but my body felt horribly cold and empty. The last thing I wanted was to go back upstairs to my room alone.

"Do you need to syphon?" Jovi asked.

I nodded, unable to hide it any longer. As soon as he mentioned it, hunger leapt up inside of me—and to my surprise, I found it drawn mostly to the energy of the Druid. There was something unnaturally bright about the aura his mind gave off; it felt different to the other supernaturals in The Shade—in some ways more ferocious and angry, but also steady, like he might never run out. Still, remembering how he'd reacted last time, and the fact that I owed him my life for what he'd just done, I turned back to Field and Jovi.

"Would either of you mind?" I asked.

"Not at all," Jovi replied, "take what you need."

I started to reach out for Jovi's energy, finding comfort in the familiar. The event had obviously shocked him—I could feel that his nerves were frayed, and that he was worried, not just about me, but all of us. I could also distinctly feel the taint of anger and dislike he felt toward the Druid, coloring his usually light and playful energy.

Taking only a little, trying to keep track of what he could

spare, I felt the warmth coming back into my body and the hunger starting to feel sated. I sighed when I took the last curl of energy, and retracted my mind from Jovi's.

"Better?" he asked with a grin.

"Much better."

I looked up to see the Druid eyeing us curiously.

"You let her take your energy?" he asked Jovi, his expression indicating that he found that extremely strange.

"Of course I do," Jovi said. "We all do."

The Druid nodded slowly, turning back to the fire to gaze into its embers. Jovi continued to glare at him.

"I understand if you don't want to go upstairs alone"— Field interrupted the tense silence that had descended— "but you still need to get some rest. I can stay in the room, if you'd like?"

"Thanks, Field," I replied, "that would actually be good, if you wouldn't mind."

"It's not a problem," he replied. "Can you stand?"

"Wait," the Druid interrupted, holding up his hand for silence. "I think your friends are waking up."

SERENA
[Hazel and Tejus's daughter]

I jumped out of the chair, the last few hours suddenly forgotten as we followed the Druid through to the next room and down to the basement. He hastily lit the lamp on the wall, and we ran down the stone steps. I could feel all of us were anxious to see them. Before we even entered the room, I could hear their breathless panting—faster than earlier, and much louder. Almost as if they were runners coming to the last stretch before the finish line.

Physically they remained unchanged. Their eyes were still closed and they lay still, but their chests rose and fell rapidly. I started to panic when it got louder still… I could practically hear the thuds of their hearts, all galloping in unison.

"Are you sure they're okay?" I asked the Druid. "It doesn't sound good."

The Druid didn't answer me. He marched over to the bed nearest to him—Aida's—and felt her forehead. He muttered something that I couldn't hear, and I glanced over at Jovi and Field. Neither of them seemed aware of the Druid's actions. Their focus was on the bodies; Jovi's hands clenched into fists at his sides, and Field's arms crossed tightly around himself.

The panting stopped. The room immediately fell silent. I took a step forward, moving in the direction of my brother's bed, but jumped back in fright as all three of them sat bolt upright on their beds.

Their eyes were open, fixed on the blank wall opposite.

"Phoenix?" I gasped, wanting him to snap out of it, to wake up from his strange state that was making me more and more petrified by the second.

"Don't touch him!" the Druid commanded me as I took another step toward my brother. Without warning, all three heads suddenly jerked upward. Their eyes rolled into the backs of their heads, showing only the whites of their eyes.

In perfect unison they spoke, their voices raspy and strange:

"We are the Oracles.

We see the past, the present, the future.

We see what is to come, and what has been before.

We see all. Time has no meaning.

In every moment, we are present in all."

The moment they had finished the last syllable, each of them collapsed backward onto the beds.

I couldn't move. I couldn't think. I just stared, dumbfounded, at my brother and friends, trying to believe that these were still the people I knew and loved better than myself, but a ringing hysteria in my mind told me that it just wasn't possible that they were.

"Phoenix?" I whispered again.

He groaned, shifting on the bed as if he was fast asleep. This time I didn't let the Druid stop me. I took his hand in mine, relieved to find that it had returned to a normal temperature. I squeezed, trying to wake him gently.

His eyes flickered open, and after a moment they settled on mine. He frowned.

"Serena?" he asked, sounding confused.

"Oh my God, you're awake," I breathed, trying to smile, to appear reassuring. I could hear the others groaning, shifting in their beds as they awoke.

"How are you feeling?" I asked.

Phoenix released my hand, moving to scratch the top of his head. The gesture was so familiar I wanted to cry with relief—whatever transformation he had just undergone, he was still my brother.

"Where am I?" he asked instead, looking around at the unfamiliar brick room and the dim lighting. He caught sight of Vita and Aida, instantly looking worried as he took in the strange hospital beds and the white sheets. He looked down at where he was sitting, blinking rapidly in surprise.

"What's going on?" he asked, his voice stronger this time.

I looked over at the Druid, but felt it was better if I explained.

"Let's wait for the others," I replied softly. "Give me a second."

I moved over to Vita. Her turquoise eyes gazed up at me in confusion, and she gripped my hand tightly.

"Serena, what's going on? All I remember is feeling sick at the party… Where are we now? Are my parents here?" she asked, looking around wildly. She caught sight of the

Druid, and shrank back a little on seeing a face she didn't recognize. "Serena?" she questioned me, her gaze wary.

I glanced over at Jovi, who was attending to his sister, then looked up at Field. I silently beseeched him to start explaining, because I hardly knew where to begin.

Field cleared his throat, and we all turned to him.

"Glad to have you back." He smiled weakly. "You've been unconscious for an entire day… We were worried."

Phoenix, Vita and Aida all looked back at him in surprise.

"A day?" Phoenix questioned.

"And a night, almost," I added, wondering how long it would be till the dawn rose. Field began to tell them what had happened. Like the Druid had done earlier, he told them the backstory first, before outlining the theory of the Druid—that they had all undergone a transformation which would now mean they were Oracles.

"Oh, come on," Phoenix burst out when Field had finished. "You can't seriously believe that—I think I would know if I was an Oracle."

I glanced at Jovi and Field.

"You did just say that you were," I replied quietly. "All of you did."

"What?" Aida interjected. "Like, we actually *told* you we were?"

I nodded.

"You all sat up and said it, at the same time. Which, by the way, was one of the freakiest things I think I've ever seen in my life," Jovi replied. I could tell he was trying to lighten the mood for his sister. I didn't think it would be even remotely effective, but at least he was trying.

"And you're the Druid?" Phoenix asked, his brow furrowing in the direction of the doorway. I could see my brother taking in the strong, muscular form of the Druid— sizing him up, working out how strong he was physically. If he could be overpowered. I placed a hand on his arm, stilling him.

"He did just save my life," I whispered quietly to my brother. "Go easy on him—I really don't think he means us harm."

My brother nodded, but I could see his jaw tightening and his suspicion growing as he surveyed the Druid. The Druid didn't seem that bothered by the intense speculation he was now receiving. He kept scanning the three of them, his expression almost pleased, as if he was responsible for bringing them through the ordeal, though I hadn't actually seen him do anything.

"I'll leave you alone," the Druid remarked. "Have some water, rest. We can talk more when you've recovered."

Great.

Another conversation on the Druid's terms. Now there were more of us, I wondered if the dynamics would start to change—if we could demand the answers we so desperately needed, rather than wait for him to dole them out when he chose to.

I looked around for water, not seeing anything.

"I'm going to get water," I said, giving Vita a reassuring squeeze. "I won't be long."

I dashed upstairs, following the Druid. He turned around in surprise just as he reached the top of the staircase.

"Serena?" he asked.

It was the first time he'd spoken my name, and it sounded strange coming from his lips. I mentally shook the feeling away.

"Water," I replied.

He nodded. "You'll find it in the banquet room."

I hurried past him, making my way back to where we'd dined. I entered the room, noticing that the plates had been left untouched, the leftover food congealing. I wondered if the Druid was the one who cooked—he must be, as I'd never seen anyone else in the house.

Taking three cups and one of the jugs that was still filled to the brim, I carried them back with me, moving slowly. A door shut at one end of the hall, past the greenhouse. I looked over, but that part of the house was in gloom. It was probably where he slept. Or perhaps he didn't sleep—he had seen or heard me in the swamp when Field hadn't… maybe he kept a constant vigil throughout the night, making sure that nothing crossed the borders that kept his home safe.

I walked toward the staircase, and rejoined my friends.

Field met me at the door, relieving me of the jug. We filled the glasses and let them drink. Vita and Aida both looked pale, Vita's hand slightly trembling as she lifted the glass to her lips.

"How are you feeling?" I asked them both when they'd finished.

Aida wiped her mouth with the back of her hand, and flopped back on the bed. "Honestly, like I've just run a marathon or something. I'm *exhausted*."

That made sense to me. Their accelerated breathing had sounded a lot like running, and even though their bodies hadn't been moving, I could feel that their energy was dangerously low.

"Do you need to eat?" I asked them.

All three shook their heads.

"I need to sleep," my brother replied.

"Not even syphon?" I asked again, thinking that was strange considering his energy levels.

He shook his head. "Maybe later," he replied, seeing my anxious look.

"There are rooms upstairs you can sleep in," Field announced. "Let's get out of this room. Not that the ones upstairs are much nicer."

They all slowly moved off the beds, Aida wobbling slightly until Field caught her, setting her up straight.

"Are you okay?" he asked. "I can carry you."

Aida shook her head, her eyes wide.

"I'm fine," she replied, looking away.

"What is this place?" Vita asked again when we arrived in the first room—the one where Jovi and I had found the Druid. The fire was still roaring away, making the room feel like a furnace after the damp of the basement.

I really didn't know how to answer her.

"Not entirely sure," I replied. "I guess the closest thing it brings to mind is some kind of plantation house from the eighteen hundreds…it's really old, but then has working plumbing and taps and stuff. Hot water as well. You'll be able to see it better in the morning."

"But we're in the In-Between, right?" she clarified.

"Yep." I paused. "I know… it doesn't make a lot of sense to me either."

"As long as there's a bed," Aida replied sleepily. "We can work out the rest tomorrow. But I'm telling you all, just for the record, I'm no Oracle."

"Me neither," Phoenix confirmed. "The only thing I can predict is that I'm going to be pissed off when I wake up tomorrow and I'm not in the fire fae kingdom."

"You and me both." Aida yawned.

I smiled, glancing over at Jovi. He shook his head in bemusement. They all seemed to be taking it, well…far better than we had done. I wondered if things would be different in the morning.

Serena
[Hazel and Tejus's daughter]

I woke with a start, sitting bolt upright in bed.

When I looked over to my left, Aida and Vita were fast asleep, Aida's curly brown hair enmeshed on the pillow with Vita's golden blonde. I sighed, feeling my heart rate slow down as I realized that both of my friends were safe.

Not wanting to wake them, I carefully slid out of the bed, pulling at the corner of my ridiculous nightgown that had gotten trapped beneath Vita's leg. I walked through to the bathroom, splashing my face with cold water. I saw my pajamas, already dry, on the back of the door. Hoping I wouldn't make too much noise, I turned on the shower, putting the water at a medium heat. I looked down at my body. My legs and arms were slashed with dried cuts from the branches and grass. I was thankful it wasn't worse. They stung a bit when I stepped into the shower, but I cleaned them off, hoping that none of the saliva from those gruesome creatures had gotten into any of my cuts.

Last night felt like one long, horrific nightmare—from the moment we'd arrived, to the creatures calling my name, and then my friends and brother sitting up with their eyes rolling back into their heads, announcing they were Oracles.

It hardly seemed believable now. The sun shone brightly through the small window in the bathroom, the air wasn't humid yet, just pleasantly warm. Keeping the windows open had also helped matters—the room didn't smell quite so musty and stale, and I could almost appreciate the shabby charm of the house. Almost.

Once I was clean and dry, I put my pajamas back on, not feeling quite as ridiculous as I had in my Victorian get-up, but close.

I ventured out of the room, leaving the girls to their sleep. They probably needed it, and I knew from many years of prior experience neither of them appreciated being woken up early. Especially not by me.

The rest of the house was silent, and I made my way along the corridor quietly, trying not to disturb anyone else. I could smell food coming from the rooms below, and headed in the direction of the banquet room, wondering if there would be anything other than last night's leftovers.

I pushed the door open, and jumped when I saw the Druid sitting at the furthest end of the table.

"Sorry, I didn't realize you were here," I stammered, moving backward out of the door. I didn't really want to be left alone with him.

"I was leaving," he announced, rising from his chair.

I looked down at the table where he'd just been sitting. There was nothing in front of him other than a glass of water.

"Don't you eat?" I asked.

"I eat. Just not right now," he snapped.

I nodded, turning my attention back to the other places that were set at the table. Once again, there were plates covered with warming dishes and a pot of something hot in the middle of the table.

"Is that *coffee*?" I asked, hardly daring to get excited until it was confirmed, while amazed to find something so mundane available on a star in the In-Between.

"Yes," he replied. "You can help yourself."

I moved closer to the pot, smiling despite myself as I smelt the warm, familiar aroma.

"Did you do this?" I asked. "I mean, do you cook?"

It was hard for me to imagine him standing at a kitchen counter, slaving over a hot stove. He really didn't seem the type.

"No," he replied firmly.

"Then who?" I asked.

He sighed, clearly unenthusiastic about having to answer more questions.

Tough. You need to start talking, I thought. We'd have a lot more questions before the day was through, I could promise him that much.

"The house. Or rather, the wards which make it safe produce all this." He gestured at the food. "The easiest way to understand it is by imagining that the house is its own 'being'—regenerating itself at the start of every day. The wards renew themselves constantly, and provide for its inhabitants."

I looked at him askance.

"And you do that? Refresh the wards?" I asked.

"No," he replied again. "A far more powerful magic is needed than anything I am capable of."

"So who then? Or what?" I asked.

The replying sigh was deeply aggravated.

"I will tell you more when your friends are here. I have no doubt that I'll be met with more questions, so if you don't mind, I'd rather enjoy my morning in peace."

"Not a morning person, then?" I replied, pouring myself coffee. If he wanted to be vague, then fine—just as long as he knew he wouldn't be getting away with it later, when he faced all of us.

He replied with a short volley of words under his breath, none of which I caught. A second later he'd left, shutting the door very firmly behind him.

Once he'd gone, I lifted up the warmer, discovering pancake-type creations on the plate. I picked one up, inspecting it closely. It looked okay—more oaty than an actual pancake. It smelt okay too, and when I took a bite, I was pleasantly surprised—as I had been with the food last night. I sat down in the same chair I'd used last night, and continued to eat and drink while I waited for the others.

I didn't have to wait long.

A few minutes after I'd finished eating, Jovi and Aida pushed open the door, eyes lighting up when they smelt the coffee. Jovi also enquired about the food and who made it, and I told him what the Druid had just told me. He seemed as baffled as I did, but didn't ask anything further when he realized that the 'pancakes' were actually good.

"How are you feeling this morning?" I asked Aida.

"Fuzzy, but still absolutely certain that I'm not an Oracle," she replied. "And pretty desperate to get out of here and back home. When do you want to leave?"

I looked at Jovi.

"I'm not sure that's a great idea," I replied slowly.

"I am," Vita announced, coming through the door. She looked around in amazement at the breakfast, but said nothing further. She came and sat down next to me, listlessly picking at her food.

Field and Phoenix were the last to arrive, the former smelling of the outdoors and fresh air. I guessed that he'd gone flying this morning. My brother looked a lot better than when I'd seen him last.

"Did you leave the grounds?" I asked Field curiously.

He shook his head. "No. I didn't want to risk it—not when we're not all together. I just circled the house a couple of times."

"But you're up for leaving?" Aida replied, her glance encompassing both Field and Jovi.

"I don't know," Jovi replied, glancing at me. "What happened last night… obviously, it's dangerous out there. We'd have to be really careful."

"But it's dangerous here too," argued Aida. "We've been taken against our will—and I know you say that the Druid thinks it's for our own safety, but do you really believe that? I mean, we don't know him—we don't know his species— we've never even heard of them. How do we know he's telling the truth? About any of it?"

"I know," I replied, "but what reason would he have to lie? He did save my life last night—that should at least give us reason to trust him a little. We know he doesn't want any of us in danger."

"But despite what he's said, he's brought us closer to the danger," Jovi reasoned. "If Azazel or whatever he's called is in *this* land, then we're in far more danger here than we would be in The Shade."

Field sighed, running his hands through his hair.

"Do you think it would be less dangerous during the day?" he asked. "From what I saw yesterday, though the land didn't look too inhabitable, I couldn't see anything lurking—and nothing saw me."

"As far as you know," I replied.

I didn't feel like leaving the house was a good idea. Not after last night. I understood everyone's concerns about staying here... but if we waited till we could find out more, till the Druid was willing to speak to us, then at least we'd be able to be a bit better prepared, and know whether or not what he'd said about the Oracle was true.

"I think we should risk it," my brother announced. "Let's find a way home, there's got to be some way out of this place. From what you've said, the Druid was able to transport us here in the blink of an eye. Maybe that means that we're closer than we think to Sherus's fire star."

Vita shook her head. "I agree with you about leaving, but as to the travel, it doesn't necessarily work that way. We don't know what abilities he has or how on earth he got us here... there might be numerous ways it could be done."

"The maps showed us a couple of cities. I think we should head toward those, see if we can find anyone willing to help us," Jovi replied. "They might even know of a portal—or we could come across some fae, willing to take us back."

I looked doubtfully at Jovi. There was a lot of hypothesizing without knowing any of the facts. But I could see I was outnumbered. None of them had experienced what I had last night, and my reluctance was hugely tainted by that.

"We all have to agree," Field announced, looking at me. "What do you say, Serena?"

Aida's eyes pleaded with mine. I could see how desperately she and Vita wanted to get out of here—and no wonder.

"All right," I said reluctantly. "We'll try."

SERENA
[HAZEL AND TEJUS'S DAUGHTER]

After we finished breakfast, we all went back upstairs to the room with the maps. We didn't see the Druid, and I wasn't surprised. I imagined that, dreading questions, he'd tried to make himself scarce.

The others discussed the map of Eritopia, pouring over its contents and arguing which way would be best to go. Personally believing that it didn't make much of a difference at this point—none of us knew what kind of creatures we'd find in the cities, or the jungle—I left them to it. I found myself wandering back into the room I'd seen yesterday, the one with the diary in the drawer of the vanity table. I opened it again, looking at the leather notebook, wondering whose it had been. Checking that no one was coming my way, I untied the leather knot and opened it onto the first page. There was no name, only a date—September third, 1805. I flicked though to the next page, feeling instantly guilty, and read the first few lines.

Same lunch again today! I curse the Daughters for not being more inventive. Almus has it far easier, being a Druid, and it is only my palate that suffers. I shouldn't complain, and I don't, not to him, only to you. But I do wonder if I will go mad here sometimes, and it is only Almus who saves me, again and again.

"Serena?"

I hastily dropped the book back in the drawer as Vita poked her head around the door.

"Are you ready?" she asked.

"I…I'm ready," I replied, doubtfully looking down at my attire. Vita's was no better—she only had a pair of shorts and a tank top, along with the fluffy robe of the palace that she'd quickly discarded once she woke, due to the heat. All the girls were barefooted, me included.

"I know." She sighed. "Not ideal, right?"

"For a jungle trek… Uh, no."

We left the room, joining the others on the stairwell.

"So what's the plan?" I asked. "What if we bump into the Druid?"

"We fight back," Jovi replied determinedly.

I bit my lip. I thought about how easily the Druid had waved away my syphoning, and fought off both Jovi and Field. I wasn't so sure that fighting back was the best option—but once again, it looked like it would be me versus everyone else, and so I decided to keep my mouth shut.

I didn't need to worry anyway. We made it to the lawn without seeing any sign of the Druid, and began walking away from the house. The grass pricked at the soles of my feet, and I winced as the blades grazed against my already cut legs.

Stop being so lame, I scolded myself. After what Vita, Aida and my brother had been though, my ordeal counted for nothing.

The ravens cried at us from above. I expected them to soar down like last time and try to block our way, but they didn't, only settling at the edge of the lawn in a single row, watching us with their beady black eyes.

Their presence unnerved me, adding to my misgivings

about leaving the safety of the Druid's home. I glanced back at the house, its grand presence looming over us. What was the greater threat? What lay within the stone walls, or what lay outside them?

We passed the ravens, and left the edge of the lawn for the swamps. They seemed just as eerie as they did at night— the moss hung still and silent, looking like hangman's nooses, the waters murky and dark. Despite the sunshine that blazed above us, the swamps felt dead and dank, unwelcoming, as if the very air warned us away.

"I bet there are midge flies here," Aida grumbled, dragging her foot from a muddy slop of land.

Field stopped us, looking up at the trees. He seemed to be the only one of our group who shared at least some of my discomfort. His eyes frequently darted around, his steps more cautious.

"I'm going to fly up," he said. "Check that we're not running into anything. I'll let you know what I see."

He crouched, then jumped up, his wings expanding as he did so, and he flew up and out of sight. I felt the absence of him, wishing that he'd remained with us below, though it obviously made sense for him to keep a lookout.

We carried on our journey. I kept a close eye on my

brother and the girls, checking for signs that they might feel faint or weak. As far as I knew, Phoenix hadn't syphoned off anyone since he'd woken up, which would be a problem if we needed to fight.

I moved toward him, matching his pace.

"Are you okay? Did you syphon yet?" I asked quietly.

He shook his head as we continued to walk side by side.

"I actually feel fine… I ate, so that probably helps. I promise I'll say something if I need to," he replied. "What about you, are you okay? Syphon off me if you need it."

"I'm fine. I'm not the one who had the weird Oracle experience," I replied.

He smirked, cocky as ever. "I think that's a load of bull. I think he must have put us under some kind of spell or something. I don't know what he wants with us, but I'm absolutely positive we're not Oracles."

I sighed, nodding. I wasn't as convinced as he was. It seemed like a lot of effort to go to, such an elaborate story to set up, if all he wanted to do was kidnap us for his own purposes. And what could those purposes even be?

As we continued our journey, Field flew down occasionally, letting us know that he couldn't see anything up ahead. The swamp was starting to turn into jungle, the air becoming increasingly humid, making it difficult to breathe. I felt perspiration covering the entirety of my body, running down my back in rivulets. It wasn't really helping my mood, and I noticed Aida struggling with it as much as I was.

"I keep daydreaming of water," she commented wistfully. "An entire bucket of it, filled with ice cubes, being dunked over my head…or a swimming pool, jumping in, submerging my entire body in cold, cold water."

"Oh, stop it," Vita moaned, hitting Aida on the arm. "Once we get further in there will be water—there's got to be a stream somewhere with this much jungle."

I hoped there was. We hadn't brought any water with us… or any food. Still, I wasn't overly concerned—in a lush place like this, water and food was unlikely to be scarce. We just had to make sure we didn't poison ourselves in the process.

We started to pick up the pace—thanks to Aida and her daydreams, we were now all in search of a water source.

"Stop, please—stop a sec," Vita called out. She had fallen to the back of the group, and I hurried to her. She bent double, leaning against a rock.

"What's wrong?" I asked, seeing her visibly pale right

before my eyes. She clutched at her stomach with an agonized groan. We crowded around her, all of us deeply worried. She had started sweating profusely, more than was normal. I saw that the hand clutching her stomach was trembling violently.

"Vita, breathe," I commanded her gently, "just breathe."

She nodded, inhaling deeply, but in the next moment her body jerked backward, her spine curving backward with her face thrown up to the sky. He eyes rolled back into her skull.

"Vita!" I cried, grabbing her before she fell.

She jerked in my arms, and Phoenix moved me aside, holding onto her tightly as she shook. It lasted no more than ten seconds, and then her body went limp.

"Vita, Vita?" Phoenix called her name, rubbing her arms to bring her awake. I heard Field land behind us, giving a sharp inhale of breath as he saw Vita in Phoenix's arms.

Slowly she opened her eyes, looking around at us all, dazed, but registering our presence.

"We need to get out of here," she whispered, her voice dry and reedy. "We need to leave… Now. We will become the hunted. His creatures never sleep."

"What creatures?" I gasped. "Who will hunt us? Vita?"

She started to convulse again, her eyes scrunched up in pain and her breathing coming out in the short pants that reminded me of when they'd all been unconscious on the hospital beds.

"Let's get the hell out of here." Field moved to pick Vita up, taking her in his arms. Before he could fly up with her, he paused, turning around in the direction we'd been heading.

"Everyone, hide!" he whispered, dragging Vita and me down into the undergrowth.

SERENA
[HAZEL AND TEJUS'S DAUGHTER]

As I ducked down, I realized what Field had been reacting to. I could hear someone, or something, running through the undergrowth at great speed, heading in our direction.

Vita's panting, and her pain, hadn't let up.

"I'm so sorry," I whispered, covering her mouth with my hand. She looked up at me in panic, and I tried to hug her at the same time, to reassure her. I couldn't let her give our position away if she cried out—I could only hope that whatever was running toward us would continue past, and that we weren't their target.

I looked over to where Aida, Phoenix and Jovi had been standing, but I couldn't see them.

Good.

Hopefully the large leaves and the bright colors of the various jungle plants would be enough to shield us from sight.

The sound grew louder. They could only be about a yard away from us now. I started praying that we wouldn't be noticed, when another noise made my blood run cold. A loud shriek, high-pitched and vicious, sounded from above us. Whatever it was, it was horrible—like an animal in severe pain. I heard the flapping of huge wings smacking against the tops of the trees.

I clutched Vita tighter, glancing over at Field, his horror mirroring my own.

The next moment, I caught sight of the creature—or creatures, as I soon realized—who had been running through the undergrowth. I now believed that they were most likely running from the creatures overhead, and so when I caught sight of them, I was no longer worried about us being found, but more worried about their fate.

They were two men who would have looked entirely human were it not for two very small horns at their temples, and slightly silvery skin, which might have just been a trick of the light. As they ran, they repeatedly glanced up into the sky, their faces fixed in expressions of fear.

They were only a matter of feet away from us when one of them collapsed on his front, a spear protruding from his back. I gasped, covering my own mouth as soon as it slipped out.

The second man flung himself down on the ground next to his companion, and before I could cry out a warning, another spear shot through the sky, landing in the second man.

I turned my head away, not wanting to see anymore.

The screams from above grew louder, almost victorious. The trees directly above us shook as wings hit against them, then shuddered still. The cries grew fainter, and I heaved a sigh of relief when I heard a final cry, coming far off in the distance.

"Are you okay?" I whispered to Vita, removing my hand from her mouth. Field motioned for us both to be quiet, pointing at the two dead men on the ground. I was about to move back up when, to my surprise, the second of the two men slowly rose to his feet with a muffled groan. The spear must have missed him by inches, its tip protruding from the earth. He stayed crouched on the floor, clutching at the lifeless arm of his companion. I caught sight of his profile, contorted by devastation.

"I'm so sorry," he whispered. "I'm so very sorry."

He muttered something else under his breath, and yanked out the spear. With a sudden explosion of rage, he snapped it over his knee, splitting it in half. Next, he took a hunting knife from a sheath at his side. He closed his eyes momentarily, his face etched in misery. In one single, fluid movement, he sliced the neck of his companion—thick silvery blood pooling out onto the forest floor.

I gasped, unable to help myself. The action had been so violent, so unexpected in his moment of mourning.

The man turned sharply in my direction.

"Show yourself," he barked out, his voice thick with unshed tears.

Reluctantly, seeing no other choice, I rose to my feet. The moment I did so, Phoenix jumped up from his hiding place, looking menacingly in the direction of the horned man. For the first time since I'd laid eyes on him, I noticed how strangely beautiful he was—unearthly handsome, like an artist's depiction of beauty, as unreal and inhuman as any I'd ever seen.

He didn't look surprised to see either of us, and less so when the others emerged from their hiding places.

"Who are you?" Phoenix demanded.

"I feel like I should be asking the questions," the man replied, his voice deep and husky, his eyes lighting on me and Aida. His stare was piercing and traveled up and down both of our figures with a lazy delight, making me feel like he was seeing right through my clothes. Vita was the last of us to stand, swaying slightly as she clutched a tree for support. The horned man's eyes widened at the sight of her, and his gaze became even more intent.

I blushed furiously, moving in front of Vita to protect her from his stare.

He saw what I was doing, and smiled broadly—the anguish of his friend's plight seemed to be momentarily forgotten and he bowed down low, not for a second removing his gaze from Vita.

"It's such a pleasure to meet you all."

I rolled my eyes in disgust. Vita just stared at him, like she was hypnotized.

"Seriously?" I interrupted. "Who *are* you—and can you stop staring at my friend like you want to eat her?"

Field moved to stand directly in front of both me and

Vita, blocking the man's view. He crossed his arms, staring him down till he replied.

"Sorry," the man replied, not sounding sorry at all. "I'm easily distracted. I'll tell you what and who I am back at the house—you've decided to abandon the Druid, I take it?"

"What do you mean?" I asked sharply. How did this stranger know where we'd come from? I glanced over at the rest of the group. Everyone—other than Vita—eyed him with deep suspicion and anger.

The horned man shrugged, seemingly oblivious to the reaction he'd just caused.

"Like I said, I'll tell you everything." He searched the sky again. "But we really do need to get moving. Unless you all wish to spend the rest of eternity with Azazel? Which, by the way, I do not recommend."

I looked to Field, wondering what he would think the best course of action was. I knew what *I* thought, that we should get the hell out of here and turn back, but I was starting to realize that my vote as the youngest wasn't going to hold much sway.

"All right." Field nodded. "We head back. But we will want answers—proper ones, not the vague half-truths the Druid provided."

The horned man eyed him speculatively.

"He may be telling you the whole truth—perhaps you just don't want to hear it," he replied softly.

Field ignored him, moving back the direction we had come. We all followed him, the horned man keeping up the rear. I kept Vita close, wondering what kind of spell he had her under—I'd never seen my friend behave so moon-eyed. He was handsome, I couldn't deny that, but her behavior made me think that something else was going on. She walked alongside me as if she was in a daze, and I didn't know how much was due to the painful episode she'd just had or the new arrival.

What I was totally sure of was that Vita had experienced a vision.

"Vita," I asked, drawing her away from the others, "what was that? Can you remember what happened?"

She shook her head, wrapping her arms around her small frame.

"I don't know," she replied. "I felt sick, horribly sick… like there was this weird bile filling up inside me…and then I saw things, like a film playing out in my head. I saw the men rushing through the forest, and that creature…the one in the sky—he had grabbed Field by the neck, lifting him up off his feet." She shuddered. "It was horrible."

I got the impression that there was more she wasn't telling me. Her face was back to its unhealthy palor, and I briefly pulled her toward me in a hug before releasing her so that we could navigate the jungle.

"It was a vision, wasn't it?" she asked me.

"I think so."

She didn't reply, staring forward as we walked. I couldn't imagine what she must be feeling—to discover that she was an Oracle, that all the Druid had said was true. I looked over at Aida and Phoenix. Would they start to experience visions soon too? Or did the Druid have it wrong, was it only Vita among us who had been passed the gift? Both Phoenix and Aida looked downcast. They had watched as Vita had convulsed painfully, they must have been wondering if they were next, and at least contemplating the fact that everything we had been told so far had a ring of truth to it.

I wanted to talk to them, but with the horned man here, now didn't feel like the right time. He obviously knew something about us, or at least our presence in Eritopia, and he clearly knew the Druid. I kept glancing back at him, wanting to keep an eye on him. Field obviously had the same idea. As soon after we'd started our trek back, he'd maneuvered himself next to the stranger, keeping his distance, but ready to attack if necessary. I wanted to know what the man's connection to the Druid was, and why he'd butchered his friend—and just left his body out in the jungle—after he'd seemed so devastated at his death in the first place.

There was also something familiar about the spears that had been shot down by the winged creatures in the sky. I tried to recall their detail, but it had been such a shock, and had all happened so fast, that I hadn't really taken a proper look at them. I tried to think why they might have been familiar to me…and then I remembered. The painting in the house—the one that had been covered by the curtain, depicting the half-man half-serpent demon riding on the back of the horse. My mouth ran dry. If those were the creatures that had been flying overhead, then we had made a lucky escape. A *really* lucky escape.

SERENA
[Hazel and Tejus's daughter]

Eventually we re-entered the safety of the lawn. The ravens were sitting where we had left them, and as soon as we stepped onto the overgrown grass, they shot up into the air, squawking and screeching, before settling onto the roof of the house.

Damn birds.

I instantly felt guilty—they had tried to warn me away the night I'd followed the shape-shifting creatures into the swamps, and their protest earlier had been a kind of warning too, but I couldn't help but be slightly freaked out by them…they were just regular birds, as far as I could make out, they weren't supposed to *know* things.

The sunshine, bright and pure now that we were out of the swamp, burned down on us from its high mid-point in the sky. I tried to wipe the worst of the perspiration off my skin, but it was pointless, it just kept coming—snaking down my back constantly. If I didn't drink a gallon of water soon I was in danger of becoming seriously dehydrated.

We all stepped through the still-smashed greenhouse door, and I idly wondered why the Druid had told me the house regenerated itself—clearly it didn't in certain respects.

Field swore under his breath. He looked annoyed to be back, mission failed and in no better place than when we started off.

"This way," announced the horned man, leading us through to the same blazingly hot room we'd first encountered the Druid. Once again, a fire was roaring away in the hearth.

"You have got to be kidding me!" I exclaimed. It had to be over one hundred degrees in here.

The Druid had been sitting in his chair, and at my explosion he stood up, looking at me as if I was insane. His eyes shifted over to his friend. His expression became questioning and he looked behind him as if waiting for someone else to arrive. The horned man shook his head. I guessed the exchange was about the other horned companion, but neither of them came out and said anything. For a split second, I thought I saw the Druid's eyes flicker to black again, but it was so brief that perhaps it had been a trick of the light.

"Well?" Jovi demanded, breaking the silence.

Once again, the horned man looked silently at the Druid as if he was waiting for permission to speak. I found that curious—was the Druid his superior somehow? They were different species, but they obviously knew each other well. It made me feel strangely relieved…sort of glad that the Druid hadn't been holed up in this house by himself. I couldn't imagine how lonely that might be—how disconnected you'd feel from the world around you.

Permission had been granted, because the horned man turned to us all, his eyes focused on me, Aida and Vita, shining brightly.

"I'm Bijarki, an incubus—if you hadn't already gathered, one of the many who live in these lands." He bowed down low, a small smile playing on his lips.

I gaped.

I'd heard of the incubi, but never come across one before—though Field might have, as GASP had rescued some incubus babies from the harpy orphanage. From what I could remember of the details told to me by my grandma Rose, the creatures were incredibly ugly, with grey, ashen skin. Perhaps that explained the silver hue he had. Talk about an ugly duckling turning into a swan… I also recalled that in myth, incubi were reported to prey on women…*huh*. That would certainly explain his behavior. I couldn't imagine it would be very difficult for a woman to fall in love—or, more accurately, in *lust*—with him.

"And the creatures above us? Why were they hunting you down?" Field asked.

"The minions of Azazel—you've heard of him?"

Field glanced briefly at the Druid. "A little, yes."

"Then you'll know he now rules Eritopia—and his minions are known as the Destroyers, particularly nasty creatures that have little in the way of a soul. They offer no mercy, and hunt only to kill, never capture." He cleared his throat—the memory of his friend's death might have been harder on him than I assumed, as his next words came out thick with sorrow. "My companion and I had displeased the

Destroyers, and Azazel himself. We were running for the safety of this house—which, I assure you, is the only place where you will have a chance of remaining alive in this land. Especially as I gather that some…all of you are Oracles?"

"Some, allegedly," Field replied.

"But we were *all* taken," I clarified, raising my eyebrow at the Druid. I wanted to know why.

"That was an error on my part," he replied evenly. "I could only sense that a few of you had begun the transformation, but as it was so early on in the process, I couldn't define which of you it was. It was better to take the risk and remove all of you than leave it to chance."

I was surprised that the Druid admitted the error, and I remained silent. I supposed if he did believe that the Oracles were in grave danger, then he'd acted in their best interests. In a way, I was glad he'd made the error, rather than just taking the three of them—it was better that we were dealing with this together, and that Phoenix, Vita and Aida hadn't needed to go through this alone.

"So what did you actually do to anger the Destroyers?" Aida asked, turning to Bijarki.

"A mission gone wrong," he replied vaguely.

I was about to interrupt, to ask for more detail on the

'mission,' when the Druid spoke.

"I need to speak to Bijarki privately. We can reconvene later," he instructed, his gray eyes gazing at us with steely determination. Clearly, he wouldn't be taking no for an answer. I would have objected—the Druid had blown us off for long enough with his requests to delay questioning— but I was so desperate to get out of the heat of the room I was glad that we could return upstairs where it was marginally cooler. I also wanted Vita to get something to drink… her color still didn't look good.

"Let's go." I turned to the others, looking meaningfully at Vita. "I think we could all use a break."

With a mutter of displeasure from Jovi, the rest of us trailed out of the room.

"I also want to show you something," I added, heading for the stairs. They followed and when we reached the second floor I led them in the direction of the painting, parting the velvet covers to reveal the image.

"Good grief," Phoenix exhaled, astonished. "What's *that*?"

"I think it's what was flying over us," I said. "Field, did you see them in the distance or anything?"

He shook his head. "Just as black dots. They must travel

fast though, because they easily covered miles in the time that I got down to you and we hid. They also came from the direction of the eastern city that was marked on the map—perhaps they live there?"

"Maybe we should be grateful we didn't get any closer," Aida replied, her wide eyes fixed on the painting. "I'm pretty positive I never want to encounter one of them as long as I live."

"Yeah," Jovi agreed. "I'm glad they weren't hunting us."

"That's the problem though," I said. "If these are Azazel's creatures, then this is what's coming for us—for you, the Oracles. If they find out that you exist, I don't think there will be any stopping them."

My brother nodded, averting his eyes from the painting and looking at me with grave seriousness.

"So what's the plan then?" he asked.

"The three of you," I replied, looking at him, Aida and Vita, "need to rest. In the meantime, we're going to get the answers we need—whether the Druid knows it or not."

Jovi grinned at me, understanding my meaning. If the Druid wouldn't speak to us directly, then we'd just have to indulge in some good old-fashioned eavesdropping.

SERENA
[HAZEL AND TEJUS'S DAUGHTER]

Field, Jovi and I crept back downstairs as quietly as we could. Using True Sight, I pointed the boys in the direction of another part of the house—an area we hadn't previously explored, which led off from the dining room. We moved silently around the banquet table when we entered, this morning's leftover breakfast things still laid out. We stood on one side of the doorway. I was closest, followed by Jovi and then Field. We stood in silence, Jovi's arm pressed against mine.

The door had been left slightly ajar, opening onto

another large room, mostly bare except for some furniture covered in off-white drapes. It faced out onto the front of the house, the sunshine only slightly shaded by a porch that must have covered the length of the building.

At the far end, the Druid and Bijarki stood in the light. The Druid leaned against a fireplace—unlit for once—his face turned up toward the sun. I could see that he was displeased about something though, his brow set in a deep frown as he listened to his friend.

"We couldn't get any closer," Bijarki was saying. "His ranks are growing though. Hordes of incubi are already swearing fealty to him...my father included." Bijarki clenched his fist, his jaw jumping. "Two of them saw us and we were chased...saw us too easily."

"You think we were betrayed?" the Druid asked, displeasure coloring his tone.

Bijarki nodded.

"They seemed to be on the lookout for intruders. That may have been a coincidence, but they shouldn't have been able to see us—not from where we stood."

The Druid turned away at this, and I became frustrated that I couldn't see his expression clearly. They both fell silent, and Bijarki started to pace the room. I jerked back, thinking that he might be coming our way, but before he reached the door he turned on his heel and paced back again. He was dressed in thick, gray cotton-like trousers, tucked into boots and a dark shirt. The clothes were simply made, and I wondered if they were some kind of uniform—they looked so utilitarian, and also completely impractical for this kind of weather. Perhaps incubi didn't feel heat the same way we did. He certainly didn't appear to be bothered by it.

"That's not good news," the Druid replied at length. "But perhaps it is to be expected. My father never could find out how far Azazel's influence spread—too many are afraid of speaking out now. He's done his job well."

"And what do we do now?" Bijarki asked. "Losing Kristos is devastating, but also problematic—we'll likely no longer have the support of his family, and lose further sway as a result."

"We wait. The Oracles are no good to us without fully developed powers. Even then, without the jinni and witch mix, I'm not sure how powerful they're going to be—what limitations they might show in their abilities."

"But surely their gift coming from the daughter of an Ancient must mean something?" Bijarki asked in surprise.

"I don't know. We'll have to wait and see."

"Well, how long? How long do you think it will take for their powers to come to fruition?" Bijarki asked again, his impatience showing.

The Druid turned to him, raising an eyebrow.

"Sorry," Bijarki muttered. "I'm worried. The Oracle is our only hope…to hear that they might not even have the powers…" He trailed off, sighing deeply.

"The sooner they actually believe me, the better," the Druid replied in agitation. "At least they now might stop trying to leave the grounds—that's one small victory. And I will help them bring the visions into being, when the time is right—"

The incubus looked as if he was about to interrupt, but the Druid held up his hand to stop him.

"It will be as soon as possible," he snapped. "Don't you think I understand the urgency? If it is a fact that all the incubi have turned to Azazel, then it will soon be over—and our chance will be lost."

Bijarki murmured something that I couldn't quite catch, but I was still reeling from what the Druid had said. I glanced back at Jovi and Field. They both looked furious. Clearly, we were fast becoming part of something that was far bigger than just our own safety—and by the sounds of it, we were in way over our heads.

I snapped my head back as footsteps moved our way. It was Bijarki, heading for the door. We all moved backward, disappearing behind the other door in the dining room. Before we were out of earshot, the Druid called out to his friend.

"By the way, Bijarki… careful how you treat the female contingent of the Oracle. Do not on *any* account set to charming them. That goes for Serena too."

"You know I can't help it," the incubus replied, barking with laughter.

We ran back up the staircase as silently as we could. We needed to find the others and tell them exactly what was going on—and less urgent, but just as important, given the strange attention he'd shown Vita in particular, I needed to warn her to stay away from the incubus.

SERENA
[HAZEL AND TEJUS'S DAUGHTER]

We woke everyone, and we all gathered in the map room. I told them, almost word for word, what had transpired between the Druid and Bijarki. After I'd finished, a shocked silence descended as my brother and friends digested the information. Jovi had started pulling out maps again—I guessed he was newly determined to find a way out of here somehow, but there was nothing in the universe that could persuade me to set foot outside the boundaries of the house.

"So we're just pawns, then?" my brother asked angrily. "He's taken us here to help win some stupid war?"

"Do you think he wants power over Azazel?" Aida asked. "It would explain why he wanted the Nevertide Oracle so badly. He probably tried to kidnap the other one the same way he did us."

It certainly seemed that the Druid's intentions weren't quite as pure as he'd first made out. It would explain why he'd brought them here at least. If he truly wanted to protect them, he would have spoken to someone in The Shade—my great-grandpa Derek, Benjamin, or my father. Told them to protect the Oracle, and to expect Azazel to come hunting. Unless he thought Azazel was too powerful even for GASP to deal with. But I couldn't really imagine that…he seemed to be some kind of demon, another supernatural like all the others they'd faced. If he knew of GASP, then he must have known of our history—the multitude of dangers the Novaks had fought and overcome.

"We don't know that," I replied to Aida. "We're jumping to conclusions. I admit this doesn't look good, but right now, what's our alternative? Go back out there?" I pointed to the window. Dusk was already falling.

"No," Field replied. "We're not going out there again— I mean it, Jovi," he added, seeing the werewolf about to interject. "We need to come up with another plan—one that doesn't see us going on a suicide mission. It might mean we need to wait for a few days, but by the sounds of it, we have time. If the Druid wants to help develop your powers, then let's let him help. If you guys can see the future, then we can use that to our advantage."

"That's a good idea," I replied. "In the meantime, I can help try to uncover his true motives. He can feel me when I try to syphon off him during the day… but he might not be so quick to react while he's sleeping."

"You're going to try to mind-meld with him?" my brother asked.

I nodded. "It might work. If he's sleeping, he could unwittingly pass on information. It's worth a try."

"I don't know, Serena," he replied, looking doubtful. "He's dangerous. We still know next to nothing about his abilities…it's a risky move."

"One I'm willing to take," I argued.

Phoenix and I glared at one another, neither of us willing to back down, and Phoenix once again playing the part of over-protective brother.

"Let me do it," he insisted.

"Oh, come on," I argued, "you know I'm better at it than you are—and much more subtle."

Aida tried to cover up a snort of laughter. "I'm sorry," she beseeched my brother, "but it's true—when you syphon it's like being hit by a sledgehammer."

Phoenix glared at her, rolling his eyes in frustration. "Fine," he bit out. "But you need to be careful. When are you going to do it?"

"Tonight," I replied.

"Someone should go with you."

I shook my head. "I'm doing it alone. It won't take long—and honestly, I really don't believe he means to harm me. He rescued me from those shape-shifter creatures. He didn't need to do that. I'm not an Oracle—I'm nothing to him. But he still did it."

"All right," Field replied, silencing my brother with a stern look. "It's worth a try. Just be careful, and don't take any unnecessary risks. I don't want him to know that we're suspicious of him, or at least any more suspicious than usual."

Plan decided, we all headed our separate ways to get some rest. None of us felt like going downstairs to eat anything—it was too hot, and I didn't think any of us particularly liked the idea of dining with the Druid and his strange friend.

Vita, Aida and I agreed to share the room again. There

were some other bedrooms, but it was better to stick together—especially if Aida or Vita succumbed to any visions in the night. I didn't want either of them going through that alone.

"I hate it here," sighed Aida, leaning her head back against the pillows. "I feel like I'm stuck in a Victorian oven. I hope our families are already hunting for us."

"Of course they are," Vita replied. "They'll have the entire fae armies out looking for us too, if Nuriya has anything to do with it!"

"I just wish we understood how far away we were from the fae stars." I sighed, looking up into the sky. "It would at least help us understand how likely they are to find us. I mean if we're deep, deep in the In-Between…" I trailed off, realizing that my speculations weren't that helpful.

"It won't matter," Vita insisted. "They'll find us."

I nodded, looking back out of the window. This was the second night we'd spent here, and our first full day. How many more would be spent here? It made me feel claustrophobic just thinking about it. My mind returned to the diary I'd found. From what I'd read, it had sounded like the writer had been stuck here too, thinking they were going crazy with the repetition of the days and the food…was that what lay in store for us? She'd mentioned an 'Almus' and I wondered if that was the same Druid, or someone else — he hadn't even told us his name. He'd been good at keeping us in the dark. I hoped that wouldn't be the case much longer.

"Are you going to sleep, Serena?" Aida asked.

"No," I replied. "I'm going to wait up… wait for the right moment."

Aida nodded, shifting on the bed to get comfortable.

"Wake us if you need to," she replied sleepily.

I went to the bathroom to get a glass of water, and when I returned, they had both dozed off.

I dimmed the wick on the lamp, throwing the room into a soft glow. Knowing that I probably had a while to wait, I decided that I could preoccupy myself with the diary—I didn't have so many moral issues with reading it now. I felt we were all desperate enough for answers that we should try getting them, whatever it took.

Taking the lamp with me, I made my way along the corridor. I didn't hear any noises from Phoenix's or Jovi's rooms and figured that Field had probably found somewhere outside to sleep again. Pushing the door to the room open, I made my way back to the vanity table, opened up the drawer, and removed the journal. Placing the lamp down, I sat on the edge of the musty bed and flicked through it, picking up where I'd left off.

This evening Almus explained the nature of his 'black arts,' as he calls it. The power of the Druids is strange to me. They are naturally much weaker than the kind I have been born to, but the way they have mastered their skills! It amazes me what he can do—he and his son, who shows so much promise. I worry about him growing up here…a lonely life awaits him. I just pray that we all remain safe. Perhaps one day this will all end—Azazel will fall, and this land will return to what it once was. Then maybe that quiet, serious little boy can experience more of what life has to offer. But it's not what I see…It's not what I see at all.

Almus gifted me an orchid. Its petals are a bright purple, its stem elegant and fragile. He told me he had been growing it in the greenhouse—that it reminded him of me.

I shut the book, feeling guilty again as the content became more personal. It did clear up a few things though—namely that Almus was likely the Druid's father. The small child must be him…but then that would make the Druid over two hundred years old. That was old.

The mention of the 'black arts' didn't sound too

promising either. What kind of magic was *that*? It sounded dangerous—nothing pure or natural like the magic I understood from the jinn and witches of The Shade. But she (and I was now convinced the writer was female) mentioned their magic wasn't naturally that strong, which was better news—though I didn't know what she was comparing it to. I wondered if the writer was an Oracle... I got the impression she had been placed in the house for her own safekeeping, and the ominous mentions of what she saw, or didn't see, made me think that she was referring to her own visions.

I put the diary back in the drawer. I would need to show it to the others, but maybe not yet. I was starting to feel a vague sense of connection to whoever had written it, though I wasn't sure why. Maybe it was just because we were both locked up in this house, but I felt like I'd almost been *meant* to discover it—like the book had been lying in wait for me.

Shaking the feeling off, I rose to leave the room. It was late, and I needed to find the Druid. Using True Sight, I searched the house, starting near the room that always had the fire blazing and then tracking along to the door at the end of the small hallway. He was there, asleep by the looks of it. *Perfect.*

I hurried down the stairs, taking the lamp with me, making sure I kept an eye out for Bijarki. I hadn't actually seen him when I'd scanned the house, which unnerved me—I didn't want him creeping up on me.

Placing the lamp down in the small corridor, I waited by the door of the Druid's room, checking that I couldn't hear any sounds coming from within. When I was satisfied, I pushed it open and silently slipped in.

There was a fire in his bedroom, only just dying down with its embers glowing. My eyes adjusted quickly to the gloom, and I could make out the sleeping figure of the Druid in bed. I watched him for a moment, noticing how different his face looked in sleep, how much younger it appeared. The blankets on the bed lay twisted and rumpled, only covering his lower half and exposing his bare, muscled chest. I recalled flying into him when I was running through the swamp—no wonder he'd felt so solid, he was insanely well-built. Unable to stop myself, my eyes ran along the narrow trail of dark hair on his abdomen, its end, thankfully, covered by the sheet.

I could feel the heat in my cheeks rising.

Focus.

I shifted on my feet, sending out the trails of my mental energy to try to latch onto his. My mind brushed against his temples softly, finding a way in.

Abruptly, the Druid shot up in bed, the surprise sending me jumping backward, my heart racing. He had yanked a huge hunting knife from beneath his pillow and he held it aloft, his muscles tensed and ready to attack.

He lowered it slowly as he realized who it was.

"You shouldn't watch men sleep," he chided me in a gruff voice.

"I'm sorry." I gulped. "I just wanted to thank you for saving my life."

"No, you didn't—you came to syphon off me."

Being caught out in the lie made me blush all the more, and I cursed myself for wasting precious moments *staring* at him when I could have done the job much faster and perhaps not been caught.

"Okay," I replied, trying to match his even tone. "Maybe I did. But it's because you're still not talking to us. You're not giving us the answers we need."

"It's because I don't know a lot of them," he replied acerbically.

"You know more than you're telling us," I insisted.

The Druid sighed, running his hands down his face in frustration. When he didn't reply, my own frustration grew.

"Listen," I snapped. "Our families will find us. We'll get out of here one way or another, and you'll have to answer to GASP. Maybe you don't think that means much, maybe you think because you're so far away it doesn't count for anything, but trust me when I say they've brought down more powerful creatures than you—including the Ancients themselves—and they won't stop until we're safe at home."

His expression changed from annoyance to pity, and his gray eyes met mine with a searching gaze.

"Turn around," he replied.

"What?"

"Turn around," he repeated. "I want to show you something—I need to get dressed."

Oh.

"Okay," I muttered, turning to face the door, feeling uncomfortable and exposed without him in my line of sight. I heard him rise off the bed and pull on clothing. A few seconds later, he was by my side, his broad frame brushing up against me as he leaned forward to push open the door.

"You're not going to like it," he muttered, leading me down the hallway.

SERENA
[HAZEL AND TEJUS'S DAUGHTER]

I followed the Druid down to the basement with a certain amount of trepidation. The house was so silent and felt even stranger at night-time than it did in the day. The lamp I had picked up again once we left his room threw shadows everywhere, making me feel like I was being watched—like something was about to jump out at me at any moment. I kept close to the Druid, not wanting to be left behind as he strode rapidly across the basement floor and over to the opposite wall.

To my eyes, it was completely bare, but he placed his

hand on a set of bricks, pushing against them. I heard a click, followed by a mechanical whir, and the wall started to part, opening up into another room.

My eyes widened in amazement as I observed its contents. It was windowless, but lights hung from the walls, making it slightly brighter than anywhere else in the house. It appeared to be some kind of laboratory; copper tables were laid out, covered with beakers and old-fashioned scientific instruments. There were quite a few potted plants and jars of herbs and other unidentifiable objects lined up against the sides of the room. In the center was a pile of ordinary-looking rocks, with a single, high flame blazing out of them steadily. I couldn't see how the flame was being maintained; it didn't look like there was anything to burn, but the flame didn't even flicker, remaining perfectly constant as if it had an unlimited supply of fuel.

"The moment you crossed into Eritopia, the protective mists that surround this galaxy caused you to cease to exist anywhere but here."

I turned to the Druid, confused by his statement. It was the first time he'd spoken since we left his room.

"I don't understand," I replied. "What mists? What do you mean we ceased to exist?"

"This land, all of the stars and planets within the region of Eritopia, are guarded by the Daughters – a group of creatures born for the sole purpose of protecting the way of life here. It is they who create the illusion—or magic, whatever you wish to call it," he replied. "It was once used to protect us all, to ensure that Eritopia remained hidden from others. Now it is used to protect others, to ensure they do not come seeking this land and the evil it holds."

"But what do you mean we don't exist anywhere else?" I asked, furrowing my brow and wondering which one of us was being dense. "Obviously we don't exist anywhere else…we're here."

"Let me show you," he replied.

He reached out his hand and waved it across the center of the flame. He didn't wince as the fire engulfed his skin, and after a few moments he removed it, unharmed. The flame started to widen, and dark shapes danced about in its center. I peered more closely, watching the shapes take form.

"It's the fire star," I breathed, recognizing the scene that the flame had produced. I saw the front of Sherus's palace, the neat lawns and stone sculptures that decorated the entrance to the fae's home. It was daylight. The debris of the party had been removed completely, and only some of the floral arrangements I dimly remembered from that night remained.

There were four figures standing on the terrace in front of the main door. I recognized Sherus, Nuriya—who was holding their baby boy—and Grace and Lawrence. Nuriya passed the child to Grace, who held it gingerly in her hands, her face lighting up as she peered down at the baby, murmuring soft coos at him and then laughing as the child grabbed her finger. Grace turned to Lawrence, and I could hear their voices as clearly as if they were standing in the room next to us.

"I can't wait to have one of our own," Grace said, smiling at her husband.

"Then let's not wait," Lawrence replied, his eyes serious and tender as he looked at his wife.

They were interrupted by Bastien and Victoria coming out of the palace, both carrying their overnight bags. They stopped to talk to the others, but I could hardly hear a word they were saying. It felt like my blood was rushing around my head so fast I'd almost gone deaf to everything apart from the panicked voice in my head that finally understood what the Druid had been trying to say.

We don't exist.

I watched as all four of them were waved off by Sherus and Nuriya, moving toward Corrine and Ibrahim, who were waiting for them, presumably to take them back to The Shade. Not one of them had mentioned us, or even stopped for a moment to look around. The Hawk brothers messed around, all looking a bit worse for wear after their night of indulgence…but they all happily strolled toward the witch and warlock, with no mention of Field.

The vision vanished, leaving only the flame, still burning brightly in the middle of the room.

"What have you done?" I gasped, turning to the Druid in horror.

"What I needed to do to keep your brother and friends safe."

I shook my head, not wanting to believe what I'd just seen. Maybe it was all a trick. Why would I trust some magic flame to show me the truth? The Druid could have manipulated the images and the voices, couldn't he? He'd mentioned illusions before…maybe this was a trick he was playing to keep us subservient so that we didn't go running off into the jungle and spoil his master plan.

"I don't believe you," I retorted, feeling sick. "This is

bull—it's impossible. You're not powerful enough, and neither are these 'Daughters' you talk about…you couldn't do this, not to witches, not to jinn. And what about the Oracle? She visited us, and you said she came here, but we all remember her!"

The Druid shook his head. "The Oracle was the daughter of an Ancient. She held within herself great power, enough to reverse the protection of the Daughters. There are no others that I have come across able to accomplish such a thing. In truth, I don't exactly know how the Oracle managed to, either."

I started to back away, wishing he would just shut up. I didn't want to listen to another word he had to say.

"I told you that you wouldn't like it, but it's true, Serena." His voice had become cold and unyielding, his face set in displeasure. "I know this is painful for you—"

"*Do you?*" I retorted. How could he possibly comprehend how painful this was?

"But perhaps it's better this way," he replied. "They are spared the pain of missing you. None of them would know you were ever born—there will be no trace of you back at your homes, no evidence that suggests you once existed."

"Is that supposed to comfort me?" I roared, rage

completely consuming me.

"Yes!" he shouted. "It is. There's nothing I can do about this, and you'll see it's better this way. Would you rather look in this flame and see your family and friends devastated?"

I was speechless. How could he possibly think this was okay? That this was a better alternative? I knew my parents, and the others. Their overwhelming emotion wouldn't be devastation—it would be determination, and they would have stopped at nothing to find us.

Now we didn't even have a chance.

"I want to get out of here," I replied, my breathing coming out in short rasps. I suddenly felt claustrophobic—the walls of the room felt like they were closing in on me, the heat feeling even more oppressive.

I turned and ran, leaving the Druid behind me. The entrance had been left open, and I pounded through it, needing to get outside of the house, just for a moment. I headed for the greenhouse, jumping through the smashed door and then coming to a stop outside. I leaned against the wall, putting my head between my legs and trying to catch my breath.

I knew I would have to tell the others. They would insist

on seeing it themselves, and I simply couldn't bear the thought of Vita or Aida seeing what I'd just seen—or Field, or Jovi. And especially not my brother.

It would tear them apart, and vanquish any trace of hope.

Vita
[Grace and Lawrence's daughter]

I kept drifting in and out of sleep. The night was so hot that I couldn't get comfortable, and Aida kept tossing and turning, making the bed creak and occasionally poking me with an elbow or leg. It was still the middle of the night, and Serena was either still with the Druid or had found another place to rest.

The heat was making my entire body itch, and so rather than try to go back to sleep once again, I got out of bed and went over to the open window. The night air was a little bit cooler, and I stuck my head out as far as it would go, smelling the sweet fragrance of the greenhouse and the overgrown lawn. I contemplated going down into the gardens, but after Serena's experience that didn't seem like such a good idea on my own. I decided I'd go and look for Serena, but first take an ice-cold shower.

The lamp was missing, so I had to rely on the moonlight. There was only a small window in the bathroom, but it was enough to see by. I ran the faucet, hoping that I wouldn't disturb Aida. I quickly stepped under the water, my body jerking awake as the cold streams smacked the heat away. It was bliss.

I closed my eyes, letting the water scatter down on my face.

Once my body was numb, I stepped out, wrapping myself in the only threadbare towel we had. I sat down on the edge of the tub, just taking a moment to enjoy the sensation of my body feeling 'normal' and refreshed before the sticky heat consumed me again.

We were all in such a strange situation. It was still making my head spin, almost like I expected reality to assert itself at any moment. This house, the Druid, the incredibly captivating incubus, the repulsive, screaming creatures that had attacked from the sky…and strangest of all, the visions and the idea that the Oracle had passed over her powers to us. How could it all have taken place in such a short space of time? How could my world, and everybody else's, have twisted inside out?

My mind drifted back to the vision I'd had earlier. It had been physically horrible—a twisting, sick feeling in my gut like I was about to vomit, my legs and arms becoming shaky and weak like they could no longer hold me up. The actual vision I'd had was even worse, more disturbing than I'd let on to Serena and the others.

I had seen the creatures Serena had pointed out in the painting, riding through the sky. The screams of their horses had been ear-splittingly loud as they had chased us. Ahead of me, on the ground, I had seen them all running— Jovi had been calling back to me, yelling at me to move faster, but it had felt like I was frozen to the ground, unable or unwilling to move. Then the vision had changed, and I was in a large room, Serena, Field and Jovi standing in front of me, their eyes wide in horror. I tried to call out to them, but only bubbles had escaped my mouth. I looked around, gasping for air as water filled my throat. Phoenix and Aida banged against a blue film that held us captive. My hair tangled in the thick water around me, winding its way around my neck, covering my eyes. I felt like I was drowning. My hand hit the wall and Serena's palm met mine on the other side, helpless to stop whatever was happening to me…and then the vision had stopped.

Enough.

I stood up quickly, trying to shake the vision from my mind. It wasn't real. It couldn't have been real.

I turned toward the small hand basin, running the tap and splashing my face and wrists with cold water. When I had calmed down, I turned the faucet off and looked up at my reflection in the small, cracked mirror on the wall. I looked pale—paler than usual, but that might have been the moonlight. Dark shadows circled my eyes, which were red-rimmed and scratchy.

A cloud moved in front of the moon, and the light dimmed. My face suddenly looked distorted. I thought it was another trick of the light, but then my reflection started to flicker and blur. I shook my head, thinking I was hallucinating. Then, backing away from the mirror, I tensed, struck by an absolute and total fear.

There was a face staring back at me.

It was a woman, with eyes that had the palest blue irises they looked almost completely white. Her hair moved around her as if it was underwater or caught in a gentle breeze—it, too, was white. The impression was like a photograph that had been in the sun too long, all of her features bleached to a strange ethereal nothingness.

The woman in the mirror opened her mouth, and I heard a voice inside my head, so quiet and breathless it was like one continual hush or whisper.

"Vita? Is that you?" the woman asked. "Can you hear me?"

I stared at the mirror open-mouthed, too shocked and horrified to formulate a reply. It took me a few moments before I could croak out a reply, but before the words left my mouth, the image started to flicker again. The woman's eyes widened in horror—and perhaps pain? The next moment, the image gave one last flicker and vanished completely.

"No!" I cried out, my hand reaching for the glass, as if I could drag her back. But she was gone, and it was only my own stricken face that stared back at me.

I stood still, panting as adrenaline coursed through me. The woman I'd just seen perfectly matched the description of someone who had been described to me countless times as a child…and the only thing that made any sense at all was that I'd somehow just managed to meet the Nevertide Oracle.

HAZEL

We said our goodbyes to my family, Corrine, Ibrahim and the rest before heading toward our treehouse. I leaned my head against Tejus's arm as we walked, relishing the peace and quiet of The Shade after the party. It had been so much fun, but in true fae style, it had been a party of excess, and though I had loved every moment of it, I was glad to be home.

"I swear Varga and Elonora have grown so fast…I keep thinking of them as toddlers," I sighed, recalling Ash and Ruby's children at the party. They had seemed so grown up—how had the time gone so quickly?

"I know," Tejus replied. "And Varga is more like his father every day. I wonder if he'd like to stay in The Shade for a while? He did mention it. Be good for him to train with Ben, Caleb and Derek. We could do with some fresh blood."

"More warriors to train?" I asked, smiling. My husband and my uncle Benjamin had done a good job at getting the Hawk boys and Benedict in good shape over the years, and I supposed it did make sense for Varga, and Elonora if she wished, to train with the others.

"Always," he replied.

We walked along in silence, my body moving closer to my husband's as I anticipated getting into our home and enjoying some alone time. My mind drifted to Nuriya and Sherus's new baby boy—how delighted Nuriya had been to become a mother, and how she deserved such happiness after so many trials in her long life.

"Tejus," I murmured softly, my heart pounding in my chest as I tried to form the words—words I had been contemplating for a while now. "I want to change. Back... I mean, into just a sentry."

He stopped walking and turned to me, his dark eyes shining.

"Does this mean what I think it does?" he asked, his hands running up my arms till his fingers brushed against the back of my neck. A delicious shiver flew up my spine.

"Yes." I nodded, biting my bottom lip as I waited for his reaction.

"Thank God," he replied, drawing me closer into his arms. "I can't wait to start a family with you, Hazel," he murmured into my hair.

He drew me into a kiss, my body crushed against his as he lifted me off my feet with the force of his embrace. My hands tangled in his hair, feeling the muscles of his shoulders beneath his shirt. I couldn't wait to start the baby-making process—I was going to love every single blissful second of it.

"So, shall we start practicing now?" he asked, breaking away and smiling down at me.

"Right now," I replied with a grin.

He carried me all the way to our treehouse apartment without stopping, but for once, even his vampire speed didn't seem fast enough.

* * *

Feeling calm and loose-limbed, I padded into the kitchen

to get a glass of water. I stretched, yawning, a warm glow spreading throughout my body as I anticipated the talk I'd be having with Corrine tomorrow. I didn't really know why Tejus and I had put it off for so long… I guessed because there was really no hurry. We had all the time in the world to have children, and it was nice to enjoy our married life together, just the two of us. But it was time. Seeing Nuriya's happiness and Ruby's—how she and Ash made such great parents—I couldn't deny Tejus and myself the same gift any longer.

Filling the glass, I turned away from the sink and looked over at the immaculate, still kitchen. I frowned. Something didn't feel exactly right. But I couldn't put my finger on what it was…perhaps something was missing? I walked into the hallway, wondering if I'd left anything behind at Sherus and Nuriya's home, but both our bags were by the door, and I'd meticulously repacked the few things we'd taken with us.

Strange.

I shrugged. Whatever it was—a toothbrush, or perhaps some jewelry—I could just contact Nuriya and ask her.

It couldn't have been that important.

READY FOR THE NEXT PART OF THE STORY?

Dear Shaddict,

I hope you enjoyed *A Gift of Three!*

The next book, _ASOV 43: A House of Mysteries_, releases **April 20th, 2017**. So you *really* don't have long to wait. :)

Visit Amazon or www.bellaforrest.net to order your copy.

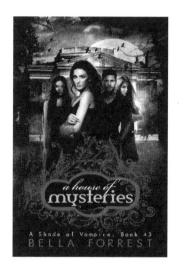

I'll see you there...

Love,

Bella xxx

P.S. Join my VIP email list and I'll send you a personal

reminder as soon as I have a new book out. Visit here to sign up: www.forrestbooks.com (Your email will be kept 100% private and you can unsubscribe at any time.)

P.P.S. Follow The Shade on Instagram and check out some of the beautiful graphics: @ashadeofvampire

You can also come say hi on Facebook:

www.facebook.com/AShadeOfVampire

And Twitter: @ashadeofvampire

Novak Family Tree

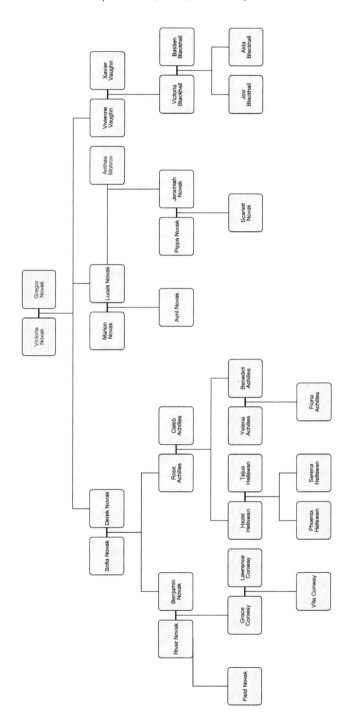

Made in the USA
Middletown, DE
08 December 2017